2145:
A Journey into the Future

by Peter Seidel

Steady State Press
steadystate.org

ISBN: 978-1-7329933-3-4 (Paperback)

Cover design by Elisabeth Heissler.

1. Science Fiction   2. Science   3. Global Warming / Climate Change

Steady State Press is an imprint of the Center for the Advancement of the Steady State Economy (CASSE), www.steadystate.org.

Table of Contents

Preface

Statistics from capable sources such as the United Nations and the U.S. government show that we are causing dramatic changes to our Earth's environment. Projecting these changes into the future shows that unless they are stopped or mitigated, we will soon be in serious trouble.

I put these grim realities in the form of a story to try and bring the world of the not-too-distant future into focus. Facts are abstract and hard to grasp. Seeing the year 2145 as inhabited by real people may help us give them some thought and enable us to process reality so we may lead more reasonable lives.

We don't know exactly what 2145 will be like. However, unless we manage to bring a sudden end to our species (not impossible), there are some things we can say about the future with fair certainty. This story is largely inspired by data that are readily available today. Those data make it clear that 2145 will be very different from 2022.

However, trends can change, and there is always the possibility of unforeseen events, so much of how things will be 123 years from now is hard to accurately depict. Projecting the future in the form of a story makes these uncertainties more pardonable and brings the data to life.

Tang

Sitting on the edge of a cliff wouldn't be particularly relaxing for most people, but Ron somehow always found it so. His home, called "Tang" after the most powerful Chinese dynasty, was an eight-thousand-acre island bounded by cliffs a hundred feet high. This allowed the inhabitants to ignore rising sea levels. They knew they'd stay high and dry, unlike the crowds along flatter coastlines who lived in fear of submergence.

Ron, a tall, slender young man with unruly dark brown hair, dangled his legs over the cliff's edge and looked down at the roiling waters of the Bering Sea. He remembered his dad telling him that their home was a newer piece of land originally created by the huge undersea volcanic eruption of 2101. Yet Tang had not transformed from a naked hump of rock protruding from the ocean to a lush environment without considerable help from the would-be inhabitants—the 100 richest families in the world. They wanted a place where they could live comfortably, unobserved by the rest of the world. Taking advantage of all the power and money at their disposal, they began a land reclamation project, dredging sand from the sea floor onto the low-lying island. Once the land mass had accumulated to a safe elevation, they hauled in freighters full of topsoil, endless sheets of sod, and ornamental trees and bushes. Then construction began in earnest: roads and walkways and docks and lavish homes. All of this occurred before Ron was old enough to bear witness.

The USA and Russia had each tried to claim the island when it first appeared, but bribes insured that the island remained independent. The island's independence made it a special place for their family and all who had been allowed to settle there. These were all "special people" as well, Ron's dad said, the "movers and shakers," political operatives and dark-money financiers that controlled—and enjoyed—most of the wealth left in the world.

Of course, a lot of helpers lived here, too: carpenters, cooks, landscapers, repair people, doctors, and house cleaners that kept the island and all its inhabitants handsome, efficient, and healthy. Ron had a couple of good friends from such families, but he had to be careful when and how he saw them, as his parents were against fraternizing with them.

Today, after his usual hour of taking in the seaside views and searching (mostly in vain) for seabirds, Ron headed back home for supper. Many of the other inhabitants used scooters, horses, or pedicabs to move about the island, and there were even a fair number of gas-guzzling cars, gone from most parts of the world now that gasoline was so costly or outright embargoed. But Ron liked to walk, for it offered him a chance to dream of the world beyond the shores of Tang.

As he came up the elaborately landscaped drive, he deduced from the extra cars parked alongside that there would be dinner guests tonight. "Off with those dirty shoes!" Lanna, the house cleaner, shrieked as Ron slunk through the doorway.

When dinner was served by Lanna's husband at the long rosewood table, Ron found himself sitting between his older sister Mauve and three of his dad's business associates. Ron's dad, Skyler Neuwirth, was a food merchant, a demanding job in a time when growing crops was a bigger gamble than ever. Even where growing food was still possible, the weather was scarcely predictable. Seasonality itself seemed uncertain. Most synthetic fertilizers and pesticides had disappeared due to economic infeasibility and, to some extent, environmental regulation (although the latter was poorly enforced). Insects—thousands of pesky varieties of coleopterans, especially—had also evolved and proliferated, resistant to the pesticides still permitted or bootlegged.

The bumper crops of the preceding centuries were long gone by this year of 2145. Ron's dad kept track of remaining harvests and moved the surplus to the most profitable places. Ron's grandfather had been in a similar business, in the days when livestock were widely marketed, and Tang still had some good-sized farms and ranchettes so that the affluent residents could enjoy the carnivorous feasts once commonplace in some parts of the planet.

To Ron's right was Rentz Trembult, Jr., one of the heads of Northland Security, a group that erected, maintained, and guarded the tall, formidable fences that separated Upper USA from Lower USA. Upper USA, sometimes called "the North," was Alaska plus the northern tier of states below Canada: Washington, Idaho, Montana, and the rest eastward to Maine. Wyoming and the northern half of Colorado comprised a special territory called Neo-Mexico, which was politically aligned with the North but administratively distinct (in some ways similar to the abandoned District of Columbia, with a major administrative presence in Denver). That left southern Colorado and the remaining states as the Lower USA—"Lowmerica" everyone called it—although the classification of Hawaii was tied up in the Supreme Court. The Northland fences prevented desperate migrants from pouring into the North to escape the humid, sweltering Lowmerica. Without such barriers, the population density in the North would increase so dramatically that the region would quickly become un-livable for all.

Sitting beside Trembult was the Neuwirth's next-door neighbor, James McCracken, a money manager who lived in a house even larger and more luxurious than the Neuwirth's. Ron wasn't exactly sure what Mc-Cracken's job entailed, but he tired of the man's bragging about his latest big deals, and the newest lavish furnishings and additions to his house, the latest being a "lapis lazuli-lined"—whatever that was— indoor swimming pool.

Next in this global chamber of commerce was Heraldine Leonard who, unlike most other denizens of Tang, traveled widely for her job. She was a geologist who searched for remaining deposits of usable minerals and metals, wherever that might take her. All the best ores and veins had been depleted long ago, but there still existed some low-grade deposits here and there, and it was her job to find them and figure out how they might possibly be extracted. As she crunched her way through a succulent salad, she shared the highlights of her recent journeys.

"I *hate* visiting Africa. You have to wear heat suits, and all the famished-looking people is a real buzzkill. But I just uncovered a vein of copper down near Cape Town, and got myself a nice little finder's fee. Plus, I was in Canada the week before—hot there too but not like

Africa—and I checked out some rumors of a potash deposit in Saskatchewan that might really help us, Upper USA at least, if we can manage to get it out of there." Nonchalantly she added, "Next month I'm supposed to go to Siberia to run down some lithium that might remain there. If it's there, I'll find it."

Ron, fork in hand, listened intently. He knew that most of his classmates at the Tang Institute, the school for island youth, were mostly interested in the parties and entertainment on the island, along with the vivid holographic experiences they regularly plugged themselves into. And the feelgood drugs that everyone on the island had access to. But Ron had always been intensely curious about the world beyond Tang—exactly what was out there in all those countries and the oceans, about which the school had taught them frustratingly little. And what were the people like out there—not just in the Upper and Lowmerica, but in all those other places where people still lived?

The children *had* learned that there was a huge part of Earth—basically all of the Tropics—that was so hot it had become unlivable. "Mesoland," the geologists were calling it, after the Age of Reptiles, because supposedly massive snakes and lizards and crocodiles had taken the place of humans. Yet there were sprawling dead zones as well, especially in the south Atlantic. Ron briefly wondered, "Wouldn't all those reptiles be moving north, too?"

The kids also knew the global population was down from the 7 billion of the early 21st century to less than 3 billion, due to what the teachers had called "global culling," which Ron suspected was a cleaner way of describing starvation, pollution, and disease; plus the loss of Mesoland to human inhabitation. Yet he wanted to see it all anyway.

Curiosity had always been a big part of Ron, and a problem for him too. It wasn't a quality encouraged on the island. He couldn't help but wonder why. The rich kids were expected to stay on the island, party with their friends, and steer clear of the helpers.

Ron's parents often cautioned him to keep his questions to himself, or at least within the immediate family circle. Now he was breaking that rule again by asking Heraldine Leonard questions about her Africa trip. Not that Leonard collaborated with the rule-breaking; her answers were evasive and, Ron suspected, intentionally misleading.

After all the guests left and the help finished cleaning, the elder Neuwirth asked Ron into his home office, an enclave near the pool with a bay window and mini bar. When Ron got there, he settled himself into one of the leather chairs, a little uneasily. His father sat across from him and broke into a speech. "Ron, you know that your mother and I really love you. We understand how different you are from your classmates and most other young adults on Tang. Your 20th birthday is coming up soon. We've always wanted to see you happy, and we'd like you to have a truly remarkable experience for this special year."

Ron held back a gag response.

The senior Neuwirth continued, "So, we've arranged for you to see some of the world beyond Tang. Hopefully that will satisfy your wanderlust enough for you to settle down here afterward. Your mother knows a couple of young ladies she'd like you to meet when you return, too."

"You really mean it? I can see the world?" Ron asked, skeptical yet thrilled by the unexpected gift.

"Of course. We've already arranged a berth for you on the *Chakirya*, from the Zipper Line, leaving port next week."

"I can't wait! I don't know how to thank you!" Ron exclaimed, as he really didn't.

"You can thank us by coming back to us a happy young man, and in one piece too," the elder Neuwirth said with a grin.

Meanwhile, on the north side of the island, in a shadowed and less sumptuous cinder block building, Lu Ming, a broad-shouldered middle-aged man with long greying locks, sat in his office chair ruminating. The young Ron Neuwirth was a puzzle. He'd always been out of the ordinary and somewhat worrisome, and now he'd be heading out into the world, potentially causing who knew what.

Ming's job was to keep things under control on Tang—and much of the world beyond it—by whatever means he saw fit. Ron embarking on the *Chakirya* certainly called for careful observation and control. The very thought gave Ming a headache, especially after a difficult month of quelling dissatisfaction among the helper ranks. Ming wondered if the sharks in the Bering Straits were enjoying the leftovers of his latest control measure.

The *Chakirya*

When the big day came, Ron was drunk with elation. He'd packed just a few things—a few outfits, a pair of binoculars, and his Tectonica for calling home and checking the *Northland News* for security reports. He arrived early that morning after saying his goodbyes, but the *Chakirya* was already there, impressively tall against the sunrise. Ron admired the ship's intricate craftmanship and its cutting-edge combination of sailing, nuclear, solar, and chem-power. Everywhere on the "zipper" were signs of old and new technology and materials. As he strode across the gangplank, plastic crates were being onboarded from a parallel plank. He descended a steep, wooden stairway to a simple but comfortably furnished cabin below deck. The room even had two small portholes, giving him a view of the surf stretching into the dissipating sunrise.

A brisk wind blew that morning and soon the ship was speeding through the Bering Sea, requiring no fuel except the wind itself. It took them only ten minutes, and they were beyond the Northland Zone that buffered Tang with a pollution-buoy system. Now they were dodging a huge mass of plastics, mingled but merged, that looked like an island of a thousand faded colors. Carcasses of sea birds and dolphins were among the flotsam, hopelessly enmeshed in the undulating panoply of plastic.

Ron knew the ship would soon be stopping at Nome to pick up more passengers, and he looked forward to their company. Any company would probably be an improvement. The crew members of the *Chakirya* seemed like a motley crew, and no other Tangians were aboard.

When the ship set to port, Ron watched at the railing as a half-dozen passengers boarded. One of them stood out from the rest, at least to Ron. He was tall like Ron, and about the same age, with curly red hair and freckles all over. He peered curiously at his surroundings as he came on board, then headed toward the short-term passenger lounge. Ron followed, intending to greet the new fellow.

Alf, the redhead, sat at one of the long picnic tables in the lounge, and took a small pouch of sandwiches out of his pack. Ron bought squid fries and a Sargasso salad from the concessioner's galley, then headed for Alf's table.

"Hi, I'm Ron. I'm from Tang and traveling for the first time. Would you mind sharing your table?"

"Why not. I'm Alf and I'm on my way home to Anchorage. Where's Tang? I've never heard of it."

Ron was surprised, as Tang would be fairly close, in Bering Sea terms. Then he dimly recalled his dad telling him that Tang was something of a secret, and that Tangians wanted to keep it that way.

"Uh, it's a fairly new place. It hasn't been settled for long, so most people haven't heard of it." Ron dodged the subject. "Is Anchorage your home? What's it like?" he asked.

"Yup, born and raised in Anchor Town. Grew up pulling the last few salmon out of the Eagle River. Ever done any fishing?" Alf asked.

"Just some surf fishing with a longline from the cliffs, but I've never caught anything like salmon. Mostly sea robins and little sharks."

The room adjacent to the lounge had some old arcade games and an air hockey table that had seen better days—way better days. Ron was amazed that a ship with such advanced technology could also be carrying such ancient artifacts, and that people would still be using them! Yet use them they did, Ron and Alf included, as the ship rocked and rolled its way to Anchorage.

As the afternoon wore on, Ron got fatigued. He

was enjoying the company though, so he invited Alf to his cabin. Alf was happy to oblige, as his own ticket didn't include a cabin.

Ron stretched out on the bunk bed while Alf took to a recliner, and they traded youthful memories. Alf pulled out a beat-up Tectonica and shared pics and videos of earlier trips. Ron couldn't help but think life beyond Tang seemed a little more interesting than his own. Hearing about someone's golf score, financial caper, or latest gem in the collection didn't stack up against running from robbers, surviving earthquakes, and visiting the Museum of Past Wildlife.

After what seemed like a forever of getting tossed about the Bering Sea and rolled around the Gulf of Alaska, they finally awoke one morning to the blaring ship horn announcing their imminent arrival at Anchorage. Ron and Alf ran to the railing and looked toward the approaching skyline—still somewhat impressive despite the rusting ruins of huge oil tanks along the shore. "Home sweet home," Alf deadpanned.

"You know, Anchor Town used to be a huge processing and storage center for oil from the North Slope," Alf explained, "and a major refueling hub for international flights. Most of the oil was gone before the end of the 21st century, though, and what little remains is stored in top-secret facilities. Only the super-rich get to tap into it. At least that's how the rumors go." Ron squirmed uneasily, knowing first-hand those rumors were true.

Soon the passengers filed across the gangplank amidst a hectic scene of laborers trundling cargo on and off, up from the holds and down off the docks. Along the docks were clusters of expectant people waiting to greet their friends and family. From the looks on the faces, Ron wasn't sure which was more evident: longing or loathing.

But aside from these standing clusters of apprehensive folks, the dock was writhing in movement. Ron stood frozen, taken aback by the hustle and bustle, the different faces and races moving off and onto ships, the beggars panning for spare change, the vendors hawking everything from seaweed snacks to Tectonica holsters to pedicab rides. Alf could sense that Ron was a little overwhelmed, so he offered, "Why don't you come stay with me for a few days while you learn the area? I can show you around some and maybe we can find a beer or two." Ron, suddenly realizing he hadn't thought about lodging—beer either—gratefully accepted.

Alf signaled to one of the pedicab drivers and gave him their destination while he and Ron piled in. Zigzagging through the streets, Ron gawked at the terrestrial sea of pedestrians, bicyclists, pedicabs, mopeds, and even mules. An electric streetcar line ran through the streets, too, but no cars were anywhere in sight. Ron asked about this, and Alf replied that, ever since the world finally reached the international "End of Oil" in 2070, no one could use cars. Electricity was reserved for more essential needs, so there was no way of fueling cars that way either. With few exceptions, the small-scale nuclear experiments had failed as well.

With a vague sense of shame, Ron didn't tell Alf about the hundreds of fancy cars parading around Tang, where the "end of oil" hadn't hit, yet.

Fifteen minutes later, the pedicab pulled up to a neighborhood surrounded by a formidable fence, complete with a sturdy plastic gate and two armed guards. Alf waved to the guards with one hand and pointed his Tectonica at the gate with the other, mumbling "open sesame" for extra effect. The gate slowly opened, as if to keep any visitors in suspense.

As they stepped along the plasti-cobbled walkway, Ron noticed his new friend assuming a different air, less cautious, like this was his turf. Alf emanated a pride of place, too. "These homes up here near the entrance aren't the best, but the ones back where I'm from are pretty good...or good enough at least!"

Three blocks in, Alf stopped in front of a large, early 22nd century style house with a smorgasbord of building materials: reinforced plastic siding, a galvanized roof with several skylights, and fabriglass windows that helped conserve energy. Above the front door was a driftwood plank with "The Strayborgs" in charcoal lettering. Alf gave a knock and opened the battened door. Like a single welcoming unit, his mother, father, and younger brother rushed forward to greet him.

"You were gone so long!" his brother blurted out while his mother hugged him tightly.

"How did the job go, son?" the senior Strayborg asked, patting Alf on the shoulder.

Alf had a degree in Resource Extraction Technology from a local community college, and he'd been sent with his extraction team to see if there might be any whales still alive in the Arctic Ocean. Supposedly the Arctic was once alive with whales, seals, walruses, and even the snow-white polar bears before they faded into hybridization with grizzlies (which were also all-but-gone now). Vague notions of somehow reestablishing healthy whale populations—renewable stores of fat and protein—had kept search parties like Alf's funded by the Upper U.S Department of Food Security. Unfortunately, they seldom had any luck spotting any whales, much less developing any kind of a whale management program. Alf suspected his crew wouldn't be funded much longer.

But now was no time to worry about whales or wages. Alf introduced Ron to the Strayborgs with a kind of flourish Ron had come to enjoy. "Meet my new friend Ron! He's from some mysterious, possibly mythical place no one's ever heard of," Alf half-joked. "I told him to stay with us for a few days while he gets the lay of the land." The family greeted Ron effusively, and Alf's mom herded them all to the dinner table.

Ron noticed that, evidently, Alf's mom did most

of the cooking herself, and even brought it all to the table. He'd seen a man cleaning the front windows when they arrived, and a woman working in the plant beds, but those were the only helpers he'd seen. It certainly wasn't like Tang. Ron couldn't recall his mom ever serving a meal; her biggest chore seemed to be ordering legions of helpers around. Ron wasn't judgmental, one way or the other, except about the food (and of that, to himself). The curried pollock with moss salad was...well, curried pollock with moss salad.

The next day, Alf took Ron to see the sights. On the way to the city center, they passed through a block of unimpressive, plastic-particle buildings with small playgrounds and an occasional patch of decorative grass.

"These are walk-up apartments," Alf explained. "You'll find these all over town. They get thrown up quickly to accommodate the hordes of people escaping that hellishly hot Lowmerica. They can't find a place to live in the Upper USA either, not the part below Canada I mean, so they take the ferries all the way up here, where Alaska lets them in for cheap labor.

"Anyway, they call these places 'walk-ups' because there aren't any elevators. The walk-ups don't have air conditioning, either. The tenants can't afford electricity. I don't know how they manage, but I guess anything is better than Lowmerica!"

As they walked, Ron noticed cameras pointed in all directions at street corners. Most were old, damaged, and probably dysfunctional, but eventually Ron noticed one with a blinking red light. Alf winked at it.

When Ron asked about the cameras, Alf responded, "Back in the 2000s, businesses installed them with government permission. They were part of an IT system, supposedly for crime-fighting, but everybody knew they were really for making money. The software could figure out what you liked and what you might buy. But after that COVID-39 crash, a whole bunch of infrastructure bit the dust. They left the cameras installed to keep people on their toes, though, and a few of them are still recording our pearly whites." He turned back for a moment and winked again as the camera blinked.

Nearing the downtown district, Ron noticed a string of newer homes, kept up nicely and neatly, almost lavishly in some cases. "Without cars," Alf explained, "there's a high demand for city-center living, so that's where all the richest people are now."

Despite the affluence in the city center, the upper levels of taller buildings had boarded-up or broken windows, signage with missing letters, and other evidence of abandonment. "Most people just aren't willing to walk more than six flights up for work or home," Alf explained. "There are a couple of office buildings a few blocks from here—for government agencies and the more profitable businesses—that use twelve stories, but those have elevators. You'd have to really be somebody to land a place there!"

Downtown, the wide sidewalks—ancient sidewalks plus edges of old streets—were rife with pedestrians. People wearing mostly patches accosted those without patches for handouts. Ron and Alf plowed their way through the crowd and into a café. Over cups of "coppee"—the synthetic replacement for nearly extinct coffee—Ron stared at the buildings and businesses around them, finally realizing what was so unusual about the sights. Unlike Tang, Anchorage was truly devoid of parking lots or even designated parking spaces. It certainly made sense, though, given the absence of cars. Pedicabs could just stop and fit in wherever they needed to. (So could mules, much to the consternation of certain proprietors.)

Across the street from the cafe, three young boys scaled the ruins of a parking garage—a mound of concrete slabs—like aspiring mountaineers. The sight made Ron realize how little green space existed in the city, with or without parking lots. The boys gave him a twinge of homesickness; he'd be climbing along his beloved cliffs if he hadn't ventured away from Tang.

As they ate their snacks, Alf started to describe the country's dire food shortage, especially in Lowmerica but increasingly everywhere. Tangians knew little about it yet, but Alf had picked up on the shortage by working for the Department of Food Security. According to Alf, it was common for people to break into fistfights over their place in line when a shipment of food arrived at a foodlet.

Another twinge of homesickness hit Ron as he thought of the sumptuous meals he'd be enjoying on Tang. Oddly, though, these twinges of homesickness seemed only to pique his curiosity further. What else would he find that would make him homesick? Why were things so different from Tang?

After a couple of days with the Strayborg family, Ron decided to move to a hotel he'd noticed on one of their jaunts. After a hearty goodbye to his hosts, he took a nearby streetcar to the Bighorn. It was one of the best hotels in the city, according to Alf, but Ron was in for a disappointing stay. The room was tiny, the bed was small, and the blankets were somehow smaller yet. There was neither a window nor a private bathroom. Clean towels and sheets cost extra after the first night. A note next to a (small) bottle of water in the bathroom indicated that more drinkable water could be found in a credit tapper down the hall. A sign on the bathroom wall warned, "Consumption inadvisable," leaving the details to Ron's imagination. A device on the slow-dispensing showerhead capped the flow at five minutes per day (probably a good thing, Ron decided, "inadvisable" sign in mind).

Before he went to sleep, Ron decided to give his parents an update and alleviate whatever worries they might have. He commanded his Tectonica to call them, and in short order it was Mom, Dad, and Ron in an animated exchange about his adventures to date. He enjoyed their conversation, but noticed some blips, some interference in the transmission. Was it simply due to the distance? Maybe, maybe not, Ron thought in equal measure. Everyone from Tang knew about Lu Ming, and Ron felt uneasy at the though of Ming listening in on Ron's candid observations of the world beyond Tang.

The Conveners

The next day, with his dwindling Tectocredits, Ron decided to find a cheaper place to stay. He didn't care for his room at the Bighorn, and he couldn't justify paying such a steep price for such poor conditions. He recalled Alf mentioning that many of the houseowners in the city accepted roomers, either for money or help.

As Ron walked along the outskirts of town, he noticed a weathered but sturdy Portlandic open to boarders. Paranoid about the possibility that Lu Ming was surveilling him, he reserved a room at the place under a false name—"Lew Mangus" he mischievously picked—and decided to grow a beard, just in case.

The owner of the house, a stout but warm-looking lady in her 40s, showed Ron to a comfortable room, complete with a crocheted bedspread and antique drawers. There was a window, unlike his room at the Bighorn, though the view was obscured by an invasive oleaster, still known in some parts as a "Russian olive" but increasingly called "bane bush" in Alaska. It seemed like half the windows in Anchorage were blocked by this insuppressible lout of the plant kingdom.

Ron's more immediate concern, though, was that he had to share a bathroom here, too. Fortunately, it was with only four other roomers instead of half the population of Anchorage, as it had seemed at the Bighorn.

For the affordable rate, roomers agreed to help with household chores. Self-conscious about his lack of experience with such tasks at first, Ron quickly developed an appreciation for the work. After a lifetime of others waiting on him, he found his chores surprisingly refreshing and empowering. He swept floors, spread compost in the garden, and led a full-on assault against bane bushes in the back yard (plus the view-stealing culprit under his window).

Ron discovered that he liked how his hands felt after a little hard work. He was proud of the orderliness he left in his wake. He wondered if this explained why many of the workers on Tang exuded a sort of quiet dignity (while most of the 100 did not).

One evening shortly after he moved in, Ron met another roomer as they tag-teamed the task of washing and drying the dishes. The dishwasher's name was Herb and, like Alf, he was born and raised in Alaska. Eager to learn more about people beyond Tang, Ron asked Herb about his schooling and job.

"I went to the state school up in Palmer, at least until I was sixteen. Then, I went to the Tectonica Corporation College—the branch in Wasilla—where I studied metal recycling," Herb said.

"Oh yeah?" said Ron. "Where do you even get the metals for recycling these days," thinking of that insufferable Heraldine Leonard and her tales of traveling to hell and back for a bit of ore.

"Well, that's a good question," replied Herb. After a moment, as if searching for metals in his mind, he anticlimactically concluded, "The best place to get decent metal is by excavating the giant landfills from the Wasteful." Ron recognized the short-hand version of "Wasteful Century," the term often used for the 21st century. "I only work in the surface levels though." Herb continued. "The real mining is done by the engineers and metallurgists coming out of the University of Alaska, where they have a program in Landfill Mining. They have a landfill survey course there, Landfill Geology 101, or something like that, where they cover some of the major landfill mining operations around the world. I knew a guy who took it and he said everybody calls it 'Wasteful Wonders 101.'" Herb folded a T-shirt. "Anyway, those engineers all live in their own section of the city called—believe it or not—Technitown."

Technitown. What a boring name, Ron thought.

He interjected wryly, "Not many Tectonica technicians in Technitown, then."

"No, no there aren't," Herb replied with the merest of chuckles and head bowed slightly.

According to Herb, science was seldom taught to ordinary citizens. Evidently the 100-guided government had decided that the sciences could be dangerous, if not downright subversive. Geology and metallurgy were exceptions, because materials like metals were in short supply and desperately needed. Producing a Tectonica (the iconic product of the Tectonica Corporation) for every man, woman, and child who could conceivably afford one entailed tons of ore and then "s'more," industry slang for landfill tailings.

As their conversation continued, Ron sensed that, aside from a few of these mining particulars, Herb didn't actually know much more than what Ron had been taught on Tang. He'd hoped to get a more complete picture of things beyond the affluent island but realized he would have to look elsewhere for this.

While Ron snoozed that night under the crocheted coverlet, Lu Ming's team worked hard to locate Ron. Ming had eyes and ears in all the hotels, but rooming houses were so plentiful and changeable, they proved harder to monitor.

Walking the streets of Anchorage, Ron discovered several parks situated between long blocks of buildings. According to the signs placed along the perimeters, these parks were created after loggers, miners, and farmers depleted the land of timber, minerals, and even fertility.

The authorities hoped a few sizable parks would satisfy the citizens' longing for the Alaska of yesteryear, or yester-century by now. Security personnel periodically scanned the scenes for squatters and looters, the latter of which were known to poach trees from the park for firewood or quick cash. Meanwhile the squatters were a perpetual problem, escaping the heat of the lower states, with many coming all the way from Lowmerica.

Ron's favorite park—despite being quite a hike from his room, and smaller than the rest—was called Valley of the Moon. There were well-kept, shaded picnic tables and benches along the walking trails, and a fast-running stream through the middle. There was even a fenced-off area for dogs to run off leash. Not that many Anchoragians had dogs since the "dogpox" epidemic of 2122 (which was actually an exceptionally virulent strain of distemper producing rabies-like symptoms in canids). Besides, most people struggled to keep food on their own tables, much less in a doggie bowl to boot. A few brave souls had taken to feeding the coyotes that occupied these citified ecosystems, though.

One day Ron even saw a rustic-looking fellow across the park, yelling through cupped hands, "Jumper! Hey Jumper!" A moment later a small coyote shot out of a clump of bane-bush and, sure enough, jumped like a giant cricket, straight onto the fellow who'd called for it. The man pulled a chunk of bread out of his coat pocket, and it was gone in a flash; a 50-calorie boost to one happy coyote.

A few days later, on his daily stroll through the park, Ron spotted an elderly woman sitting on a bench, staring at a thick stack of paper, seemingly bound together with a spine, opened somewhere near the middle so the papers were splayed out in either direction. Was this...a book?

Ron had seen pictures of books on his Tectonica, and some actual items in a protective glass case at the Tang Museum of History, but he'd never held one in his hands. All the reading he'd ever done was on the backlit screen of a Tectonica or Tectonica II (the larger version for home use). It worked okay, yet he was attracted to an actual book the way a foodstop microwaver might be attracted to an old-fashioned cooking stove. So, he approached the woman, fixated on the book, but once he arrived at her side, he was lost for words. "Hi, I'm sorry if this sounds strange, but do you mind if I look at that... that book?" The thought briefly occurred to him that this may have been the first time in his life he'd used the word "book" in conversation, which explained the slight stutter in his enunciation.

The woman's furled brow—a mix of caution and confusion—slowly transformed into a soft gaze and finally a generous grin. She pushed her long grey hair from her face, a face wrinkled with age and maybe wisdom, and neatly arranged the loose strands with a few colorful clips. Struck by Ron's innocent-looking face and genuine interest, the woman handed him the battered copy of *Bivalves of Alaska* after dog-earing her page.

"Wow, this is incredible!" Ron enthused. He paged through the book, peering at the printed pages and marveling over the glossy inserts displaying colorful clams and mussels. Disarmed by his appreciative response, she introduced herself as Megan, a former professor of ecology.

Ron inquired about her education. She'd been educated at Rutgers but moved northwest when New Jersey became unbearably hot and increasingly inundated by sea-level rise and hurricanes. She kept moving further and further northwest, not liking anywhere enough to stay until she was all the way to Anchorage. She took a position at the University of Alaska, and eventually ended up a tenured professor in the Department of Ecology. Before she reached retirement age, though, the infamous curriculum downsizing of 2125 took place, and she was out of a job, along with most professors outside the Department of Geology and Mining, the Economics Department, and the Business School.

"Why did they get rid of the ecology department?" Ron inquired.

"They got rid of a lot of departments during the downsizing. Today, the government only cares that we learn how to locate more resources, run a business, or grow the economy, but colleges and universities used to have courses on everything imaginable: writing, art, chemistry, sociology, history, languages, philosophy, astronomy... The sky was not even the limit! And yes, there were great programs in ecology. Of course, those were changing rapidly because of all the ecological unraveling that came along with global heating."

Ron detected a melancholy tone, and Megan seemed in a far-off place for a moment, perhaps because of the ecological unraveling.

Megan recovered and continued, "The mission of most universities was to stretch minds and teach students how to think, not what to think. Nowadays, the remaining higher-ed institutions just help people prepare for jobs, and really specific ones at that."

Ron knew from her answer that Megan was precisely the kind of person he needed for answering questions that had nagged him for years. The two of them moved to the shade of a sycamore tree, and Megan continued with her perspective and expertise. She told Ron about some of the profound environmental changes that had taken place so far in the Third Millennium: the melting of the polar icecaps; the near disappearance of Florida to sea-level rise; the conflagrations that had burned over a billion acres of boreal forest in Canada and Siberia; the extinction of thousands of species including the iconic polar bears, gorillas, and elephants;

the frightening development of Mesoland. Almost everything could be attributed to human activity; in particular the skyrocketing economic growth that plagued the planet since the 20th century, with its relentless greenhouse gas emissions and devastating ecological footprint.

There were natural disasters that exacerbated all these problems, too. In 2054, a massive eruption of Mt. Merapi split Java in two and caused a tsunami that killed nearly a million Indonesians on Java and Borneo, causing mass emigrations and triggering a civil war in Malaysia. Closer to home, the Tectonic Turbulence of the 2120s wreaked havoc along the subduction zone in southern Alaska, wiping out a swath of IT infrastructure and giving rise to the opportunistic Tectonica Corporation rooted east of Denali. And of course, the violent weather flowing from a heated lower atmosphere remained a source of controversy for much of the 21st century. How much of the havoc—tornadoes, hurricanes, torrential downpours—was caused by GDP growth and how much was truly "natural?"

By the 22nd century, anyone privy to a science education knew the score: GDP and global heating were the driving forces behind the increasing frequency of disastrous weather events, along with the more grinding, omnipresent forces of sea-level rise in coastal areas and droughts in expanding deserts. Yet uncertainty persisted among the masses, just as the Tangian cabal preferred.

Megan explained that those in power disliked science, except for sciences with a practical purpose or potential for profit like industrial technology. The elite had no use for the humanities and natural sciences; business was everything. Their concern for the future was limited to growth projections and bets that the coming years would return to them more than they invested.

Megan described how nearly a third of the USA was almost as unlivable as Mesoland now, primarily due to global heating, lack of potable water, and widespread toxic waste. There was insufficient cropland, and weather conditions were no longer suitable for growing wheat and corn. The wheat belt was now up in the Canadian plains, whereas in North Dakota, Minnesota, and southern Wisconsin, plus the Palouse of Idaho and Washington, farmers had resorted to growing millet, spelt, and teff, grains that could take the heat and make it through some of the lesser droughts. However, much of the land was badly deteriorated, and the agricultural surpluses of the 21st century were long gone, so only a much smaller economy could be supported.

Megan was really on a roll now, moving from the ecological to the economic and social problems of the 22nd century. "By 2100, human labor was replaced by robots in the service sectors and 'dumbots' in the manufacturing industries, leaving hordes of adults out of work. Competition for the remaining jobs was fierce, and the pay went down to subsistence levels. A lot of people surrendered themselves into servanthood for food and shelter. 'Volunteer slaves' they're called. Others—way too many—made a living out of crime. In 2108 there were over 200,000 homicides in the USA, mostly in Lowmerica but plenty in the North too."

Despite the horrific topics, Megan appreciated having such a rapt audience, as Ron sat motionless on the bench for an hour, hypnotized by Megan's fountain of knowledge. When Megan noticed the long shadows and dimming light, she stood to return home.

"I've bent your ear enough, but if you haven't had your fill yet, I'm part of a small group you might enjoy." Megan's mood seemed to lighten now as she continued, "It's quite a cast of characters—some past professors, workers that got replaced by robots, and couple of resource extractors, one guy that even used to make Tectonicas—and we get together once a week. If you'd like to join us, meet me here next Wednesday at sunset and we'll go together."

"Count me in," Ron replied with palpable enthusiasm. "I look forward to it! Do you have a name for that group?

"Of course we have a name. We call ourselves the Conveners. We don't have a mission. We don't have a political party. We just explore and we convene to do so. We like to think that, if two heads are better than one, a bunch of heads are way better. So, we're the Conveners."

Ron liked the idea and was excited to test it out with "the Conveners." As he bid Megan farewell and walked deeper into the park, Ron encountered crowds of people surrounding a woman shouting from atop a plastic picnic table. "God is punishing us for our sins by heating up the world. Come to our daily services at Church of the One True God and be redeemed before the impending rapture. If we join together and change our wicked ways, God will heal our planet and provide a bounty for us all. Those who refuse to join us will be left behind to get what they deserve!"

Responses filled the air around the woman, and most were negative. The booing was loud and there were sarcastic retorts like "Sure thing, Lady Moses!" Yet the would-be prophet had her supporters, too. Some carried signs with doomsday slogans like "Mesoland is Coming" while others shouted "Allahu Akbar!" through cupped hands. Confused and increasingly uncomfortable, Ron squirmed his way out of the crowd and practically ran the whole way back to his room. He suddenly wondered if "convening" was always a positive.

Regardless, a week later Ron met Megan at the park bench as instructed, careful to avoid the area of the park where he'd encountered the prophet and her feverish audience. Megan was sitting on the bench waiting for Ron when he arrived. She led him ten blocks beyond the park to a modest A-frame shrouded by huge oaks.

Without knocking, Megan turned the plastic doorknob and ushered Ron into the home. Seated around a spacious room, seven open-minded savants discussed what was going on in Anchorage and beyond. They aired their concerns about the changing world and brainstormed ways they might prevent further devastation.

Clara was a 90-year-old former history professor. She'd actually taught at Washington University in St. Louis before Lowmerica was fenced off. As the oldest member of the group, Clara was able to share first-hand accounts of a time that would have been inconceivable to the others. She frequently added to their discussions by describing major changes that had occurred during her lifetime.

Amos was a streetcar conductor by day, a sculptor by night, and a socialist throughout. He was the group's political zealot, ready to trace the roots of all evil to "capital" and, especially, "capitalists."

Martha had been a psychologist decades before. She liked to remind the group that, unfortunately, most people wander through the world thinking at a very shallow and primeval level, susceptible to the guile of salesmen and politicians. No one in this group argued to the contrary (although one or two wondered about the irony of that).

Ben was a grizzled 60-year-old managing a foodlet owned by a subsidiary of Tectonica. He disapproved of the subsidiary and the mother company, but he needed the T-credit. A self-described history enthusiast, Ben read everything he could find about the past, a hobby hamstrung by the proliferating advertising online and the extinction of libraries and bookstores.

Shirley, a thin young nurse with a mess of curly black hair, was disturbed by the callous way medicine was practiced. Despite her youth, she believed in developing a more equitable healthcare system that prioritized people over profit. She'd seen the corruption of the industry firsthand and erupted into frustrated rants when people asked about her field. Even Amos backed off when Shirley got rolling.

Bert had taught high school English literature until the subject was deemed unnecessary. Then he spent years struggling to find steady work, doing odd jobs to make ends meet, mostly in landfill resource extraction. He slept many a night in parks or abandoned buildings, fairly safe as he had essentially no possessions to attract a thief with. Some of the group suspected Bert of convening just for the crackers that eventually made the rounds, but Bert was articulate, nonetheless.

Julia was the youngest member. An enthusiastic blonde with green eyes, she loved the outdoors, especially birds. She never tired of the starlings, sparrows, and juncos flitting about the Anchorage parks, even among the dense stands of bane bush. Zoology courses weren't offered in schools anymore, so Julia spent her free time learning about wildlife by perusing old articles and videos online. To earn a living, though, she managed a computer program for Fantaste, a grocery chain found in Seattle and Alaska.

Ben, the foodlet manager and designated discussion leader, started the meeting with an update on a missing member, Jason. An engineer in the prime of an enviable career (financially at least), Jason had been working on a water project in the Potholes, an extensive area of erstwhile tundra in the Tanana Valley, when he'd contracted hantavirus, evidently from a woodchuck burrow his crew had to excavate. After a few weeks of debilitating pain, Jason had died two days before the meeting.

"Oh no, our poor Jason," Clara the elder said mournfully, clasping her hands near her heart, head bowed, grey hair falling as if to signify the entropy that overcomes life. As the closest one to death in the room, she spoke for the group on this. Besides, no one else really knew what to say—for the time being at least—so they moved on to Ron.

Ron got their minds at least partly off the demise of Jason, albeit unintentionally, when he told them he was from Tang. The group was dumbfounded; none had even heard of Tang despite their far-flung knowledge of Alaska. Once he described it, though, a few members looked as if Ron had confirmed a long-held suspicion of theirs.

Ron was suddenly on the hot seat of a lengthy inquiry, fielding questions about his home despite his lingering concerns about Lu Ming surveilling him. He even dared mention that Northland Security was headquartered on Tang. Right about then, he had a fleeting sense of irony over the thought of Ming, as the proceedings felt like an interrogation at times.

"This explains a lot of what's been going on." Amos nodded but immediately wanted more. "Alright then, young man. Tell us exactly where Tang is. Is Tectonica up there too? Who else besides Northland?"

"What do you all do with your money and power?" asked Bert, the one furthest from money or power.

"What kinds of food do they eat up there?" Ben the foodlet manager wanted to know.

"Yeah, what kinds of food?" echoed Julia, the youngest and hungriest.

Ben said he'd once come across an old T-site that explained how the planet's richest people just vanished from the public eye. He'd been skeptical when he first read it, chalking it up to the vivid imaginations of conspiracy theorists. Now, he wondered what other "conspiracies" he'd disregarded as fiction.

After one of the most exhaustive (and certainly the most exhausting) discussions Ron had experienced—as the central discussant no less—he revealed beyond a doubt what they all suspected already. "The people on Tang are running the world, but I'm starting to think they know very little about it, or what the people are dealing with outside of the island. Making money, staying in power, and a life of luxury is all that really matters to them." Amos the socialist nodded most approvingly, but no one disagreed, either.

Clara, with her unmatched life experience and historical knowledge, started somewhat empathetically, "People have different goals and interests. Some are curious and want to learn, some want to improve society and those around them, some want to create, and some simply want to accumulate money and power." Her observations became less conducive to empathy as she added, "Unfortunately, those who have the most typically want more of it, even if it comes at the expense of the masses. They can't seem to nurture a conscience about the future generations, much less the other species."

"Those with the money and power view themselves as important, even elite, because they're among the few that have achieved this, which they wrongfully assume is everyone's goal," Martha psychoanalyzed.

Ben put it in simpler terms, "The few who run everything don't care as long as they're making all the money." Then he veered toward the topic of bad governance. "Throughout history, humanity has been cursed with bad governments run by the ignorant, the greedy, or both. Tang sounds like the current version, that's all. I'd say we're pretty lucky to host a fellow who knows about the place first-hand. Thanks for finding him, Megan."

Ron felt like a living, breathing conversation piece, which he was. No one acted threatening, though, or even very judgmental, and he readily agreed to become part of the group, at least during his stay. The group was invigorating for Ron after a lifetime of superficial conversations on Tang. Conversely, Ron had helped to reinvigorate the Conveners, too, and as they dispersed, everyone looked forward to the next meeting.

It would be dangerous to speak one's mind anywhere else.

Julia

Ron was eager to learn more about the mountains he'd heard about at the meetings. He'd always been aware that mountains existed—had even seen T-sites and videos of them—but now he'd have a chance to actually visit one. He mentioned his desire to visit one to Megan, and she enthusiastically agreed to fulfill his wish.

"There's all kinds of mountains around here, but since you're new at this, and my knees aren't what they used to be, let's pick an easy one. We can save Denali for another time! Let's do Flattop; the peak is just over 3,000 feet. We can actually take a shuttle to the trailhead right from the middle of downtown."

They met again at their favorite park bench the next morning. Ron, heeding Megan's advice, wore long pants and sunglasses. She had a bright red bandana tied over her hair and carried a pack with two bottles of purified water and some snacks. The mule-drawn shuttle was crowded and noisy, but soon enough they were off-loading at the trailhead.

The trail quickly became steep and rocky, but Ron and Megan were able to maintain a decent pace. In some spots, plastic stairs had been built into the mountainside to aid climbers.

"These mountain meadows off to the side were once covered in spectacular wildflowers," Megan said, "but when it got hotter—even at this elevation—most of them were replaced by invasive weeds, and others were poached for camas roots." Ron noticed the meadows seemed to have more litter than flowers, invasive or otherwise.

Reaching the top was worth the demanding climb, though. Ron had experienced panoramic views from his cliff on Tang, but there was little to see but sea. Now, in every direction, he saw rolling hills, rushing rivers, and the occasional wildlife roaming the terrain. The sky was big and blue; only dotted with tufts of cloud.

Ron could see Anchorage and a tantalizing view of Cook Inlet, along with mountains upon mountains: the Chugach Range, Alaska Range, Aleutians. Megan pointed out the famous Mt. Susitna, or "Sleeping Lady," as well as Mt. Einstein, one of the smaller peaks she was especially fond of. "It's only 11,400 feet high," she sighed.

"Shouldn't they have picked a bigger one for Einstein?"

Ron only inquired, "Who's Einstein?"

Megan ignored the ignorance and lamented, "You know, Ron, the Chugach Mountains were home to more than 50 glaciers back in the Wasteful. They were the last resort for a bunch of endangered species, too, that got pushed off Earth with global heating. Well, global heating plus the plundering for food and firewood by Homo sapiens. 'Homo scrapiens' I call 'em sometimes, scraping out every last nook and cranny for food and fiber and firewood. So now it's these hideous 'haircuts' as far as you can see," Megan expostulated, sweeping her arms in a broad arc over the western horizon. She was pontificating, but she was right, too. The hardwoods had been cut as fast as they could grow in the lower elevations, leaving mountaintops of scraggly "piss fir" in every direction. Pine and spruce had long been squeezed out, ecologically by hardwoods below and economically by plastics in the markets.

After some time for Ron's soaking in of the besotted vista, Megan offered, "Imagine what all this looked like centuries ago. It would have been gorgeous beyond imagination and brimming with natural riches!"

Ron couldn't quite imagine it, though. He really had no idea whatsoever what vast forests of spruce and pine below blue-white glaciers and sawtooth peaks might have looked like. Just a moment ago he'd been fairly impressed with topography alone, plus the toupees of subalpine fir adorning the less craggy mountains. Now, with Megan's admonition in mind, he couldn't help but wonder what he might have missed. This particular wonderment would pester Ron for the rest of his life. What had he missed?

Ron and Megan holed up at the Flattop Flopover hostel and returned to the city the next day. With the mountains mostly out of sight and mostly out of mind, Ron mostly enjoyed a long walk to the southernmost stretch of Anchorage. It was late afternoon when he arrived at the doorway of a café adorned with a sign that read, "Live Alaskan Steel Band." Listening for the band, he heard instead a chaotic cacophony a few blocks away. Against his better judgment, but in support of better-yet curiosity, he headed toward the noise, which soon included sirens.

Running now towards the action, Ron came upon a billowing cloud of dust at a heap of rubble. A harried woman with olive skin was fleeing the scene, shaking her head, and shrieking, "Another one!" Victims lay on the ground, thrashing and bleeding, while EMTs gradually phased into the scene.

Another one? Ron remembered the rumors that occasionally a building outside of Tang—and not just an old one—would give way and collapse. Wanton recklessness had come in the wake of the wantonly Wasteful Century. The City of Anchorage, for example, claimed it couldn't afford the building inspections required for safe construction in areas of prior permafrost, even though it funded the legal fees of an oil company claiming a right to keeping its name (ConocoPhillips) on the rooftop of the tallest building in Anchorage.

High-rise buildings had collapsed thrice in 21st-century Anchorage, and Ron had appeared just in time for the most recent episode. He'd helped here and there, searching through rubble for survivors and escorting a bewildered child to safer ground. But 23 people had died, and dozens of families were cast into chaos. Ron read about it two days later on his Tectonica.

There was a similar problem—a safety problem— with food. There weren't enough food inspectors, and rules weren't enforced, so suppliers simply sold what would make them the most money. Food poisoning outbreaks were common, and Megan had lost two friends in the horrible 2138 outbreak of botulism when a truckload of dirty, hastily stored carrots was unleashed upon an unsuspecting marketplace near the Valley of the Moon.

Schools and hospitals did the best they could to address the food-safety threat by using lab animals— mice primarily—to test any fresh produce headed to the cafeterias. Many a mouse met its demise in a dingy food-testing lab of the Russian Jack district. Megan said she used to oppose the use of lab animals but was left ambivalent about it after the botulism outbreak.

Thinking about animals, Ron remembered that

one of Julia's favorite attractions was the Alaska Wildlife Conservation Center, a sanctuary for wounded and disabled wildlife. The center sounded interesting, and Ron saw it as an opportunity to get to know Julia better. Megan expressed her approval with a twinkle in her eye, and Ron called Julia via Tectonica. Julia, shy as she was, agreed to the excursion, attracted as much to the conservation center as to Ron or a date.

Friday morning at 10 sharp, Ron knocked at the door of Julia's rooming house, a down-at-the heels, fully (and fully faded) plastic flat subdivided into apartments. But despite the warped porch railing, cracked sidewalk, and poorly fitting front door, Julia emerged pristinely dressed and groomed as though she lived in a Tangian mansion. Embarrassed, she apologized for the building's unkempt exterior. Rooms for long-term rent had been hard to come by, she said, and her salary wasn't up to much more.

The conservation center wasn't exactly close, but the walk gave them a chance to chat. Though it took a little prodding, Ron eventually got Julia to open up. He wasn't a charmer like Alf, but Julia liked his even-keeled style. After a while, she'd talk at length, which Ron appreciated; the more she talked, the less he'd be subjected to revealing his luxurious upbringing.

It struck Ron that the two were coming from opposite ends of an embarrassment spectrum; her from an embarrassment of poverty and he from an embarrassment of riches. Well, opposites were supposed to attract and, so far so good.

Julia was an only child, she said, flicking a wind-blown lock of hair. (Most children were, with the one-child restrictions in Upper America.) She grew up with pets, which helped explain why she loved animals so much. Her family cherished them even when they (the pets, not her family members) might have supplement-ed the meager stewpot ingredients. They raised a coy-ote-collie mutt—"Mutter" they called him—a cat miss-ing a front paw, and a couple of egg-laying hens that doubled as pets and protein providers.

Though Tangians were partial to miniature dog breeds, Sphynx and Scottish Fold cats, and Tennessee Walker horses, Ron admitted he had never owned a pet.

The conversation lulled, but luckily Ron and Julia were just arriving at the conservation center, a sprawl-ing complex that, according to Julia, had grown much larger in recent years, partly due to the extinction of businesses on either side (one an old gas station, the other a butchery). A tall, friendly docent in a green vest greeted them at the gate and gave them a tour of the grounds. Once mainly devoted to rehabilitating wildlife from oil spills, vehicle collisions, and bullet wounds, the center had developed a more comprehensive conserva-tion mission. The old butchery had become the head-quarters of Extinction Reversal, an organization loosely rooted in a 21st century movement called "Extinction

Rebellion."

Extinction Reversal put on educational programs, mostly on the T-net, and managed a DNA bank for preserving the genetic identity of imperiled species, in hopes that eventually the species might be regenerated by cloning, captive breeding, and "rewilding" their ancient stomping grounds. The green-uniformed man read off a list of the candidates consigned to the DNA vaults: Caribou, musk oxen, wolves, mountain goats, beavers, bald eagles, Arctic fox, osprey, and even giant halibut. Neither Ron nor Julia knew it, but the menagerie was sort of a who's who of 20th century charismatic megafauna from boreal and Arctic regions (none of which had a snowball's chance in hell of reoccupying significant terrain on 2145 Earth, with its carbon load of 670 ppm.)

Impressed and encouraged, Ron and Julia went to visit the animals in the many rehab pens and tanks on the property. Julia led them to the fox impound first, telling Ron how she made a monthly contribution to the care of one of them. Though they weren't quite sure which of the half-dozen foxes across the fence was "Doobie," her adoptee, Ron left the area inspired by Julia's devotion to the critters.

Moving into an area with smaller pens, they saw a raccoon with three legs, a blind rabbit, a coyote missing half its lower jaw, and a woodchuck of undetermined trauma. Finally, they visited a small apiary with a maimed owl, a red-tailed hawk with charred tailfeathers, and a crow with one wing. By the time they exited the apiary, the mood was more melancholy than the one Doobie and his fellow foxes had briefly imparted.

On the way home, Julia tentatively outstretched her hand and Ron instinctively took it. He needed it. They both needed it. It was as if the melding of their hands might make the coyote's face whole again, in their minds if not in the cage.

After a month of exploring Anchorage, sometimes holding hands with Julia and once on a beer run with Alf, Ron felt he ought to continue his mission of seeing as much of the world as he could. Strict border control meant leaving the USA wasn't an option, though. Even nearby Canada was fenced to keep Americans—all of them and not just the Lowmericans—out of Canada's own troubles.

Shirley had suggested Seattle, Missoula, and Minneapolis, where she knew some people who might be helpful. As part of Upper USA, each of these options were legally open to Ron and readily reachable with his father's travel allotment. The Conveners were sad to see him go, but each and every one of them envied him the trip, and all wished him well.

Julia, though, had a third emotion as well. She and Ron had been spending more time together, and she seemed to be... she thought she was... she surely was... falling in love. Ron probably was too, although he seemed further detached from his own feelings than anyone she'd ever met.

For his part, Ron wished Julia could come with him. But he also knew she couldn't leave her job at Fantaste—jobs were crucial off Tang—plus he didn't want to expose her to whatever dangers the journey might pose. He really cared about Julia.

Meanwhile, Ron was concerned about Lu Ming's monitoring. Purchasing passage to Seattle, he adopted the alias "Ted Tolzien" and boarded the zipper ship *Sandra Lopez*. His fellow passengers included Native Americans traveling to Tectonica-sponsored pow wows and business meetings, king crab prospectors with more prospects for whiskey than crabs, loggers weaned off Sitka spruce and now settling for pole pine, miners trained in Landfill Geology 101, foodstop microwavers in search of higher-paying foodstops, and rare tourists like himself. There were even six members of a religious group dressed in distinctively drab ("olive or olive-green?" Ron wondered for the briefest of moments) clothing. They isolated themselves to one corner of the ship, though they weren't reluctant to proselytize to anyone in proselytizing distance.

The *Sandra Lopez* (named after a two-term governor of Alaska, 2060-2068) stopped at a few other ports and docked for a day in Sitka, where many of the Native Americans disembarked for business-meeting purposes.

Ron eagerly took the opportunity to stretch his legs and see the city. He was astonished to learn that Sitka was the largest city in the USA by area, totaling almost 5,000 square miles. And, unlike southern coastal regions—Florida being the posterchild for land loss—Sitka was actually accruing acreage due to "isostatic rebound," a slow-motion bounce-back of land once held down by Pleistocene glaciers.

There was so much ground to cover in so little time that Ron hired a horse cart. He saw Aleut totem poles and reconstructed longhouses, Russian Orthodox churches-turned-museums, and ruins of fish-packing plants and Sitka spruce sawmills.

The cart driver, a brusque and disreputable-looking character in a ragged jacket, told him that the halibut and crab stocks in the area once seemed inexhaustible, but it turned out they weren't. Similarly, the once-magnificent forests surrounding the city had been turned into pulp-pine plantations to build cheap homes and provide the paper products needed by immigrants and non-immigrants alike. Sitka had also been a regular stop for cruise ships, but those days unofficially ended with the sinking of the *Sitkantia*, which went down in the Fifth Pacific Hurricane of 2094. By now, Pacific hurricanes were commonplace and had generated their own naming convention, similar to that of the South Atlantic and Gulf of Mexico. (With most of the Pacific hurricanes originating in Russian or Chinese waters, the next one up was "Konstantin.") Ron thanked the cart driver and gave him a tip, calibrated roughly to the character's character.

Back on the *Sandra Lopez*, Ron relaxed in his cabin and called Julia to report on his Sitka experience. They went into video mode, and she showed him her new haircut. There was nothing not to like, and in return, Ron modeled the newly clean-shaven look he'd returned to for his "Ted Tolzien" persona. They shared a short laugh and a lengthier smile, as Ron floated toward Seattle.

Containerville

As the *Sandra Lopez* entered Puget Sound, Ron was overcome by a stench just before huge pockets of debris appeared off port and starboard, bobbing at the water's surface. The stench stemmed primarily from a dead sea lion entangled in an offshore wind-turbine cable but was supplemented by a thousand mini-stenches from the debris. Ron heard someone matter-of-factly inquire, "What the hell is that?" All in all, it was an inauspicious, stenchful entry to the Sound.

As the *Sandra Lopez* zipped into port with her plastic wheelhouse and her 22nd-century mix of wind, solar, and wave-conversion power, Ron saw evidence of a city trying to stay above water. This was no Sitka, elevation supplemented by isostatic rebound. On the other hand, neither was it New Orleans, fully submerged after a futile century of fighting off a rising sea level. Seattle was somewhere in between, literally and figuratively. The uphill neighborhoods were no problem, but the city was struggling mightily to maintain its iconic docks and Pike Place shoreline.

Seattle was the northernmost Upper American city of truly huge size below Alaska. It came into prominence as a transport hub for supplies en route to Alaska and the Yukon during the Klondike Gold Rush, so it had a long head start. Its ample moisture and relatively mild weather made it the fastest-growing city in the USA throughout the Wasteful. It had grown since then, too, due largely to the ecological infallibility of Lowmerica and partly to the influx of Lowmerican escapees. The huge population, however, meant a large homeless population. Displaced Seattleites were everywhere peddling whatever wares they could drum up, and otherwise begging for spare change.

Rains in the Puget Sound region had become much heavier since the Wasteful, causing flooding problems in the city and washing away whatever remained of the salmon spawning grounds higher in the watershed. The disappearance of snow and ice from nearby mountains had not only put an end to winter sports but, more importantly, had drastically reduced the summertime water that farmers depended upon for their crops. The prices of potable water rose to premium levels, too, despite what seemed like more water than ever in and around the city. The profound distinctions among fresh, brackish, and saltwater were not lost upon Seattleites. In many ways, ecologically and economically, Seattle was at the leading edge of global-heating science, and its citizens learned quicker than most about the causes and effects of sea-level rise, "migration" of flora and fauna northward and upward, and the conflagrations that charred vast acreages of the Pacific Northwest.

Ron hailed a bright blue water taxi drifting along one of the city's canals and asked the paddler to take him to the shoreline hotel district. There he found an available room at one of the grand old guesthouses, the Fairmont Olympic. He planned to stay at least until he could meet up with Shirley's friends, John and Susan Noble, deeper in the city.

The Fairmont had once been one of the most luxurious of Seattle's hotels, if not of the entire Upper USA. A fancy, beautiful, and antiquated place, only the bottom few floors were in use. The lobby had threadbare carpets, the pool was no longer in service, and the signature white columns of the façade revealed patches of peeling paint. The central location was still perfect for an explorer like Ron, though.

Ron decided to venture out on his own for a day or so before reaching out to the Nobles. He noticed a tour-guide service advertised in the lobby, so he called and reserved a personal tour of the city.

His guide, a willowy woman named Sarah, picked

him up in front of the hotel in a pedicab. Their first destination was the heart of Seattle, where many of the city's most famous companies were headquartered. These included BuyAll, BestAll, and other T-net-based "Best" companies, including Amazon Best, which delivered innumerable products with a fleet of drones ranging from tiny to near-helicopter size.

The "Best" companies were all headquartered in the taller, well-kept buildings. Sarah said they still employed a fair number of people, locally and remotely. The T-net was "alive" and well, although there had been some tense moments near the end of the Wasteful when frequent flooding in the USA and a period of slippage between the Eurasian and Pacific tectonic plates in Russia wreaked havoc on infrastructure.

Yet the Global Chamber of Commerce spared no effort to repair it all, as the T-net was not only the primary means of communication, but also of conducting business, including the massive business of entertainment. The GCC knew that a population preoccupied with amusing themselves was less likely to fret about "sustainability," "social justice" and the like. The right kinds of entertainment kept people in consumption mode. Besides, if you were inside and online, you weren't suffering outside in the heat!

Sarah stopped at the corner of Third Avenue and Cherry Street to show Ron the nine-story building constructed in 1916 for the Arctic Club, a group of miners and land speculators who'd struck it rich in the Klondike Rush. By the 21st century the building had become a luxury hotel, and even now, the third floor was adorned with a long row of terra-cotta walrus heads. "You don't see that every day!" Sarah factualized.

Ron had a faint suspicion of the factoid's irrelevance, yet he had to concur, "No...no you don't." He suddenly wished Alf was there to chime in irreverently with something like, "No shit, Sherlock."

Sarah braked for a minute near the city center to point out the arresting architecture of the "Pulmonary Branch" of Virginia Mason Medical. It was established precisely in 2100 to treat the victims of smoke inhalation, as seemingly endless wildfires east of the Cascades sent suffocating smoke into the city. Many of the patients here would never breathe normally again, she said, but thanks to the Pulmonary Branch, "they can at least breath abnormally."

"All is relative," Ron added, after a phrase he'd picked up from the Conveners.

Sarah next insisted on taking Ron to the Space Needle, the iconic symbol of Seattle that had withstood almost two centuries and a gazillion tourists since its erection for the 1962 World's Fair. "By the end of the Wasteful the Needle had fallen into disrepair due to lack of government funding. The people of Seattle—volunteer carpenters and metal workers and painters—took it upon themselves to save it." Sarah's pride of her fellow Seattleites was palpable. She led Ron up the many graffitied flights of stairs—the only way to the top— and they were rewarded with a breathtaking panorama of the city, Puget Sound, Mt. Rainier, and the Olympic Mountains. While a dense raft of debris was visible on the Sound, the vast distances helped to hide the ecological unravelling of the previous two centuries. Invasive species, endangered species, and re-shuffled species were out of sight and out of mind. (Many were out of memory by then, anyway.)

Not far from the Needle, a huge open-air market had everything from fresh vegetables and fruits to shoes and clothing, housewares, and furnishings. "Over here, Ron...I want to show you something." At a table covered with small plastic bowls, she picked up a brightly colored teff bowl, turned it upside down, and put it just below Ron's face.

"Wow, made in China?!" Ron had heard of a certain level of "global trade" (not to be confused with the one-way collection of international curiosities on Tang) and here was evidence, assuming the manufacturer was legitimate. For the most part, global trade was seen as an economic artifact from the depths of the Wasteful, when it had contributed to "milking the planet dry" as some critics described it. But Ron could see how it might have excited people, as his curiosity was piqued by the thought of the plastic around him originating across the Pacific Ocean.

While plastic had largely taken the place of wood, metal, and stone in the construction and fabrication industries, even plastic production was no mean feat. The best plastics still required petroleum of some nature. The only thing that had saved the industry was the process called "plastic particulating," which allowed for the use of the crudest of oils, including partially filtered shale and tar-sand oils that were unfit for much else. The process allowed for ingraining "particulates" from the shales and sands into the plastic stock, resulting in plastic products that, while not particularly durable, were readily reproducible (so far).

But plastics could only hold the attention for so long, and soon Ron found himself buying a pendant of polished petrified wood—the state gemstone, no less—that he thought Julia might like. Then, two stands away, he purchased a Yakima hand-woven scarf for his mother, even while wondering if he would ever see his parents again.

As they went from the city center to the surrounding areas, Sarah explained that there had been a great need for new housing to accommodate the hordes of people fleeing Lowmerica. Single-family houses had become exceptionally expensive, so most of them had been replaced with apartments and row houses. The city itself, now densely populated, was surrounded by abandoned suburbs where many old homes and department stores sat deserted and deteriorating. Given the rarity of fossil fuels, charging electric vehicles was too expensive to allow for much commuting. There wasn't sufficient sunlight for solar powering vehicles, either. In the few suburban areas where public buses still ran, tiny homes were packed along the routes.

Like Anchorage, Seattle did have many parks. However, the parks were thoroughly overrun by the homeless. Sarah gave him a whirlwind tour of one park, Golden Gardens. A sign at the entrance read, "Golden Gardens: Sand, Sun, and Surf." While Ron found no evidence of gold or gardens—and only a hint of sunlight—there were certainly plenty of homeless Seattleites wading in the shallow surf with the sand, which made for a muddy mess along the shore.

As she pedaled her guest—her employer for a day—back toward the hotel, Sarah pointed out a barge inching along the canal running parallel to Elliot Bay. "It's slow and low-tech, but what a great way to move the heavy stuff. Once the barge is loaded, a single horse or mule can move it without any fuel except oats or hay. I've also seen them use a team of horses to get one moving, then unharness one horse to team up for the next barge while the other horse pulls the first barge. Kind of like the changing of the guard.

The barge was encouraging to Ron. It was indeed "slow and low-tech," but perfectly effective. After all the harsh realities Ron had discovered since leaving home—environmental, economic, and cultural problems galore—the sight of the barge lifted his spirits.

"There's one more thing you need to see before we get you back to the hotel," Sarah said. She then pedaled him across a bridge of the canal to a downtrodden area where huge rectangular boxes filled an entire city block. "This place is called 'Containerville.' The people living here took the metal containers once used in global trade and repurposed them as homes. If anybody tells you, 'Watch out for the boxers,' they're talking about these folks. They've been known to steal a thing or two, and they can get pretty rough. Don't go walking through this place alone, especially at night."

Ron noticed small chimneys on some of the box houses, and some had "windows" of thin, more-or-less transparent plastic. The doors were vintage; about as secure as you could get, Ron thought. The area gave off a dour ambience, yet there were signs of hope and aspiration, too. Plastic children's toys lay around half the houses, and little plots of flowering weeds, cultivated for effect, adjoined a few. It was a good observation to end the day with, and a tired Ron was glad to be back at the Fairmont. "Thank you so much, Sarah. You were a great guide and I'll always remember the tour." He gave Sarah the fare, and half as much again, shocking her with the level of generosity.

The next day, when Ron finally picked up his Tectonica and called the Nobles, he learned that John and Susan had a daughter; only one, of course, pursuant to the law. John was in the shipping business, which was now conducted partly by electric trains fueled by wind turbines. Susan, on the other hand, used her advanced robotics training at one of the tech companies. Since these were open-minded friends of Shirley's, they made excellent conversationalists for Ron, who was relieved to hear that the Nobles would come to the hotel the next morning for coppee. He appreciated a day of relaxation.

At the coppee shop, it didn't take long for Ron, John, and Susan to find common ground and intellectual stimulation. Ron was still curious about the nauseating smells in and around Puget Sound. The Nobles explained that the Sound had once been a beautiful body of water, but gradually became a dumping ground as regulations were loosened to grow the economy during the Wasteful. Hard as they fought, environmentalists just couldn't prevail over business interests, and the city government (as with seemingly all city governments) was essentially business interests. Money was what mattered, so it was money that won. Waste—including some highly toxic forever chemicals—was scattered everywhere, and it all went downhill to the Sound.

A particularly nasty problem was the storage tanks at old nuclear power plants. Seattle had two such old plants, each of them built in the 2180s when local, state, and federal governments pulled out all the stops for GDP. Unfortunately, these governments turned out to be poor planners for the storage of spent uranium, and eventually disagreed about where to store the uranium and which agency was most responsible. The City of Seattle had sold out and accepted a federal "ransom grant" (as labeled by environmentalists) but made the idiotic choice of storing the waste along the north edge of Containerville, presumably for lack of political power among the boxers. To complicate matters, the containers used to store the uranium resembled the old global trade containers, but looked newer, and therefore more attractive to the boxers and their children, many of whom also needed boxes. Now the city officials had an extra security problem to deal with, and without extra funds to do so, having taken the ransom money and ran.

Ron was no nuclear scientist, but like most people, he knew that nuclear waste was extremely dangerous and depressingly long-lived. That night he had a nightmare about boxers with four arms and green, glowing eyes, pushing boxes off barges, stealing barge-pulling horses, and generally running amuck among the increasingly radioactive neighborhoods of Seattle. At the end of the dream Alf appeared, yelling "Let's get the hell out of here!" as he and Ron ran in and out of a hopelessly expansive maze of box homes full of nuclear waste.

Ron awoke sweating, fists gripping the plastic bedpost. Gradually he let go, got up, dressed and headed down to the coppee shop. Then he arranged for a pedicabby to bring him to the Nobles residence, which thankfully was up in the Stevens district, far from

Containerville (but still not far enough from the nuclear waste, when Ron really thought about it). Under the Nobles' porch awning, Susan was frowning into her Tectonica. "Hi Susan. What's wrong?"

"I'm so disappointed." Susan sounded sad. "Seattle was always so progressive and open-minded, but with so many people flooding in from Lowmerica...the stress is really showing. Now apparently, there's a big crowd at the Space Needle protesting the city's refugee policy. Look, they're shouting, 'Seattle for Seattleites!'" Ron could hear the chants alright, clear as a whistle from the late model Tectonica.

"Meanwhile," Susan continued, "there's another mob of mostly immigrants coming down from Kerry Park. They're shouting, 'Learn to share, Seattle!' The riot police are trying to keep them away from the Space Needle crowd.

"I don't know, Ron. I don't even know what to think. I do want Seattle to share—John and I want to share—but where does it end? Pretty soon Seattle won't be Seattle anymore. It's already nothing like it used to be; not even close to how it was before the Wasteful.

"Meanwhile those hypocrites in the city government; they want Seattle packed to the gills with consumers, but they're ensconced up in Hawthorne Hills, behind their stone walls and security fences. They want the rest of us packed in like sardines, while they're up there eating the last of the salmon."

Ron was puzzled. "I thought the Washington State border was shut to Lowmerica."

Susan clarified, "It's supposed to be, but Seattle has a 'business exemption' and escorts hundreds more every night in wagonloads. They start out in Portland, come up through Longview and Olympia, and they're here in 15 days. Some of them—the best and the brightest—go straight to work up in Hawthorne Hills, but most of them are thrown to the wolves at South Park or Sand Point. 'Good for GDP,' the city council says, when we need more GDP like we need...more boxes of nuclear waste at Containerville."

"We sure don't need that!" a tired Ron heartily concurred. Yet his thoughts shifted quickly to a problem of another kind. He could have sworn he was followed on his way to the Nobles. The same short, stocky, plainly dressed man with a brown suitcase showed up in his peripheral vision on three occasions. Twice the man was looking at Ron before quickly turning away; the third time he was on his Tectonica. Could Lu Ming somehow have tracked him here? Ron couldn't imagine how that could happen...unless the *Sandra Lopez* subjected its passengers unknowingly to facial recognition software as they boarded.

Perhaps it was time for "Ted Tolzien" to change his appearance again and move on to another city. Ron decided to start re-growing a beard the following day, buy a pair of clear, oversized glasses, and dress more like the locals. Then he'd be on his way to Spokane.

He'd return to Seattle when the dust settled a bit; then back to Anchorage...and Julia.

Gutierrez

John dropped Ron off at the train station for his 1,300-mile trip to the "Mile High City." John was quite familiar with the train system, as his job included coordinating freight train shipments. He warned Ron to keep his pack close to him at all times on the ride—including in the sleeping compartments—and asked him to keep in touch. After getting his ticket for the 24-hour trip, Ron thanked John for his hospitality, climbed the plastic steps, and found a window seat on the north side of the train, from which he could look north, if not quite yet in longing.

Soon the train was rumbling along through the drought-stricken countryside in the middle of Washington, stopping briefly in Spokane, where a sign near the station proclaimed: "The Birthplace of Father's Day."

Pressing a button on the seat-back in front of him revealed a few other interesting facts about Spokane. It was a trapper's paradise in the 19th century and an important rail and mining center in the 20th. In the Wasteful Century it was christened "the scam capital of America" and considered one of the likeliest cities in which to have your car stolen. That wasn't much of a problem in the 22nd century, as you were unlikely to have a car.

Spokane had several vineyards and two microbreweries, so Ron bought a beer from a burly vendor during their brief stop in the city. It was a dark brew and wasn't bad, despite being warm and mostly hidden in its plastic bottle.

By the time Ron finished his beer, the train was winding through tunnels in the mountainous country to the east. Ron admired the view of the mountains from his seat, despite all the dead pines and spruce and balding mountainsides. It reminded him of Anchorage; here too stands of deciduous trees were taking over the ancient boreal highlands, where pine and spruce had succumbed to global heating, bark beetles, and catastrophic fires.

The train zoomed into Coeur d'Alene, Idaho, where Ron bought another beer; this one a rich yellow pilsner called "Old Ukraine." "Old" was more apt than "Ukraine," since Ukraine was fully merged with Russia a century prior. Either way, Ron enjoyed the beer, which came in a real glass bottle and tasted grainy. By the time he finished it, darkness was setting in over the high Palouse.

When it was finally too dark to see out the window, Ron headed for the sleeping berth and called Julia on his Tectonica. She told him a fox had died at the conservation center—she chose to believe it wasn't Doobie—and Ron told her of the three coyotes (one was actually a wild dog) he'd seen from the train thus far. Wildlife was their go-to topic, much as weather was to most.

"Oh Ron, just take care of yourself, ok? I'm worried about you getting into trouble. You're such a nice guy; people will take advantage of you if you're not careful." Ron, with two beers under his belt, rolled out the "H" word for the first time, "Honey, I'll be fine," choosing not to worry her about Lu Ming. "You be careful too and say hi to Doobie for me." He slept well that night on the rolling train, thoughts of Julia rolling along as well, now and then punctuated by the train whistle.

The next morning, a voice on the intercom announced that the train would soon be stopping at West Yellowstone, the exit point for people who'd won the lottery for visiting Yellowstone National Park. Only twenty million visitors per year were allowed; about half came from the East and half from the West (of Upper USA). The train would stop for three hours of maintenance, loading of supplies, and boarding of passengers. Ron would get a chance to stretch his legs and do some exploring on foot.

Even Tangians knew about Yellowstone. Famous as the first national park in the world, Yellowstone had long been the crown jewel of America's National Park System. It was the largest nearly intact natural ecosystem in "Old America" (the one-time 48 contiguous states) during the 20th century at almost 3,500 square miles. Yellowstone had provided a safe home for hundreds of species of mammals, birds, fish, and reptiles. Though most were long gone with the ancient glaciers and climate, a few holdovers remained, including pronghorn antelope, mule deer, and black bear. As much a sign of global heating as the disappearance of bighorn sheep was the appearance instead of javelina, which now were found in pockets throughout western Lowmerica and parts of the Upper USA as well.

Yellowstone was in neither Lowmerica nor the Upper USA, not fully at least. Parts of it were in Montana and Idaho (Upper USA) but most was in Wyoming which, along with northern Colorado, comprised Neo-Mexico. Neo-Mexico was a political bow to the old state of New Mexico—"Old New Mexico" as it were—most of which was now below the Mesoland Containment Corridor, and therefore outside of any American jurisdiction or administration. In other words, most of the original New Mexico had been forfeited to the ecological chaos of Mesoland, with most of its inhabitants fleeing to the Neo-Mexican lands of Colorado and Wyoming.

The constitutional and political categorization of

Neo-Mexico was confusing to everyone from Santa Fe to the Supreme Court. Historians viewed it as the "New New Mexico" politically, but in terms of its governance, as a bit of a fallback to the 19th century notion of "territories." Demographically it was 91 percent Latino (of mostly Mexican and Guatemalan origin). In any event, all of Yellowstone was administered by the National Park Service, as if it were in the Upper USA.

Yellowstone still had lush forests—albeit mostly deciduous now—free flowing rivers, and the extraordinary geothermal features that stirred fears of evil spirits among its earliest human visitors. Ron had always dreamed of seeing Yellowstone. Most of the other national parks had long ago been transferred to developers for mining and logging by the powerful land barons of Tang.

Bicycles were available for rent next to the train station, so Ron rented an e-bike, bought a map of the park, and headed to the Old Faithful Inn. He felt the heat as he pedaled and noticed some surprisingly bare areas along the road; areas that seemed unlikely to ever have hosted elk and moose, much less bighorn or mountain goats. He did see a mangy coyote and a scrawny mule deer, and the inn had a twenty-acre pen with five bison mulling over their daily drop of spelt hay.

At the entrance to the inn, under an imprint of the Department of the Interior's bison mascot, was an educational display:

What you see in Yellowstone today is not the way things were hundreds of years ago. As the planet heated—especially from the mid-20th century on—the park experienced far less snow and far fewer days of freezing temperatures. Snow had been a cornerstone of regional ecology for thousands of years. Less snowmelt in the spring altered the watercourses, the fish and amphibians in them, the vegetation in the park, and even the migrations of mammals and birds. Many native plants died or were crowded out by invasive species that could better withstand heat and drought. Populations of most large mammals disappeared by the 22nd century. What remains are mule deer, whitetail, pronghorn antelope, and black bears. Javelina may also be sighted, as their range has expanded from the South.

Some jerkerino had scraped at the word "South" with a knife and scribbled with a marker "Lowmerica." Ron hoped the Park Service could fix this blight on the otherwise tasteful display, but he doubted it could be fixed, much less soon. Furthermore, he suspected the park rangers may have conspired to leave the display defaced, as a monument to the stupidity of visitors.

Ron really wanted to see Old Faithful in action—it was still on its almost hourly schedule—so he ventured no further. He had a spelt burger at the outdoor cafe, saw the geyser erupt, drank some of the best water he could recall (bottled matter-of-factly as "Yellowstone Springwater"), and pedaled back to the train station.

As the train sped away from Yellowstone and headed south, he cheered up a little at the sight of the Grand Tetons in the distance, even without their once famous snowcaps. Most T-sites of the Tetons showed them bare, as they almost always were now, and 22nd century explorers like Ron didn't know what they'd missed. So, Ron was inspired by the peaks, but just before the train approached the railroad bridge over the Buffalo Fork, Ron was startled by a sudden screech of brakes. A few passengers lurched onto the floor. The engineer had done his best to stop short of a pile of logs right before the bridge, and no one was badly hurt.

Once the train stopped, everyone rushed to the windows. A half-dozen men, carrying assault rifles and handguns, ran toward the front of the train. Two of them restrained the engineer, while the others jumped up into the first car, the VIP car. Soon they reemerged pushing a handcuffed couple ahead of them, followed by a Latina maid carrying a set of young twins. The captive man tried to fight back, but was immediately pistol-whipped for his trouble.

"By God, there goes another family!" said a grizzled traveler next to Ron. "Goddammit, there's just too many kidnappings up and down this line, and the bandits are getting bolder all the time."

"You mean this happens a lot?" Ron was amazed at what was unfolding, which seemed like the scene from a video game he'd seen on Tang. "Who does this kind of thing?"

"These burnt-up hills got plenty of desperate people. They figure there ain't enough food and water, and it ain't shared fair and square, so they aim to even things out."

Ron couldn't help but wonder, based on the tone and tenor of the explanation, if the commentator next to him had a tinge of desperation himself. He checked for the can of pepper spray in its holster as furtively as he could. John Noble had gifted him the spray and holster on their way to the train station in Seattle, and insisted he wear it throughout the ride.

"Well, what happens to the captives then?" Ron wondered aloud. He could see the kidnappers and captives piling into a pickup truck; most in the back and a few in front including the maid and twins.

"If they're lucky, their relatives will pay the ransom. If the relatives don't pay up... well then goddammit, they'll end up in some box canyon, as skeletons." The commentator was loud, almost yelling, and other passengers were watching him now. Ron thought he spotted one of them checking furtively for a pocketknife or something of that nature, presumably.

The truck tore off down a dusty two-track, and after a minute, most of the passengers got out to help clear the logs from the track. The engineer, shaken but not injured, called the Blackrock station with his Tectonica, inspected the bridge, climbed back aboard the engine, and got the train rolling again.

Ron was glad he wasn't in the VIP cabin and could only hope the bandits weren't high-tech enough to be aware of his Tangian origin. His imagination was rolling now, rolling along with the train, and he wondered if Lu Ming would stoop so low as to tip off the bandits.

As this and other conspiracy theories came to mind, for Ron and other passengers too, the train persisted to Cheyenne, the Old-West-flavored capital of Wyoming. Cheyenne had once been the largest city in Wyoming, and part of a huge, heavily populated, economically developed area stretching all the way to Pueblo, Colorado, called the "Front Range Urban Corridor." From what he could see of Cheyenne out the window, Ron thought it might be a ghost corridor now. Parts of it looked absolutely deserted.

Soon the train was clickety clacking its way through the last mountain passes to Denver itself; a Lowmerican city legally accessible from the Upper USA only by rail. Denver had been called the best place to live by *US News & World Report* in 2016 and was one of the fastest-growing cities throughout the early Wasteful. Alas, this state was no longer the "cool, colorful Colorado" it once was. Colorado had heated up more than much of the country due to its continental coordinates. The heat in Denver was exacerbated by 100,000 acres of pavement and its pockets of concentrated economic activity.

By 2145, Denver had lost most of its peak population and people were still moving away as the climate got drier and hotter. Summer temperatures were dangerous for people, especially for the very young, elderly, and ill.

And of course, Denver got few protections of the American government, consigned now to Neo-Mexico. That said, it was better off than Lowmerican cities, due to the heavy presence of federal facilities and agencies rooted in the 20th century.

Ron felt the scorching heat the moment he stepped off the train in the early afternoon. He soon developed a headache and even some dizziness; a sensation he'd hardly ever experienced. After walking for a while in the blazing sun, his shirt was plastered to his skin and his shaggy brown hair dripped salty sweat into his eyes. His mouth felt dry as cotton. Maybe he'd had one too many beers on the train ride, and not enough water; his calves cramped up if he stopped to rest. He bought two large bottles of water at a sidewalk stand, drinking one immediately and pouring the rest over his head.

Tourists and especially the locals watched in astonishment because water wasn't cheap: almost $90 per bottle! The price reflected the bouts of inflation toward the end of the Wasteful, when the USA tried "solving" limits to growth by throwing money at the problem, inflating the money supply in successive waves until the Federal Reserve was dissolved in favor of the First Bank of the Upper USA—a bona fide central bank.

Meanwhile, Denver was getting most of its water from mountain snowpack as it melted each year. Once the snow was gone, not only the prized Colorado skiing disappeared, but so did the city's water supply. Inflation struck from the supply side as well. These twin forces of inflation—"demand-pull" and "cost-push" the economists called them—struck nowhere harder than in the water sector of the drying West. In fact, water wars were breaking out all over the world, including the USA. Residents of desert regions like Sonora, Arizona, and Southern California had been artificially supported by water from the Colorado River and eventually the Mississippi, but supply lost the race with demand long before 2100.

Global heating and its effects on rainfall added to the water shortages of the Intermountain Region. That part of Colorado east of the Continental Divide was even drier than the West. To add frustration to inflation, rains in the upper plains were often far too hard. They'd become monsoons, causing flooding, erosion, and pulses of pollution that compromised the potability of canal water and even well water. Yet when the clouds weren't bursting, they rarely yielded rain at all, so droughts and grass fires scorched the watersheds and left them prone to further erosion.

To top it all off, the Ogallala aquifer had been pumped dry by 2045—a century before Ron's arrival in Colorado—reducing the agricultural potential of eastern Colorado to cotton and hemp, plus a few pockets of teff along the South Platte River. As for wheat, only a tiny pocket (winter wheat only) was grown in the basin where the old John Martin Reservoir had silted in along the Arkansas River.

Most houses and businesses stood empty now. Folks who remained in the ghost towns were more ghost than folk. Denver itself was half empty, and the remaining population was 68 percent Mexican. Most of the rest were Latinos whose ancestors were squeezed out of Mesoland by the sheer inhabitability of its heat, humidity, and reptilian dominance. In the tricentennial year of 2176, the U.S. government (in the throes of splitting into Upper America and Lower America) quietly gave up on distinguishing among "Mexican Americans" from Mexicans per se in the Lowmerican states.

Ron had nothing whatsoever against Mexicans or Latinos at large, but he hated the heat and depauperate conditions of Denver. If it had a redeeming quality, it was bike-friendliness. Denver had been left with long, wide ribbons of pavement charging off into every direction, plus a beltway encircling the core. Ron's hotel, "Beltway Beds Southeast," offered a full selection of rental bikes. It was conveniently positioned near the southeast corner, allowing the early-rising Ron to ride north with the sun at his back, all along the city's eastern flank. It was still hot, but much more bearable than his mid-afternoon jaunt the day before.

Even better, Beltway Beds had franchises at each

corner of the beltway, allowing Ron to break up his ride into four stretches ranging from 18-26 miles. The first two stretches—heading north and west—were bearable if not refreshing. Ron found that coasting the bike wherever he could had the effect of cooling his sweating skin. Days three and four—south and east and largely into the sun—tested Ron's endurance, as he drank $740 worth of water! At the end of the trip, back at Beltway Beds Southeast, the temperature at 108°F, Ron called his father on the Tectonica and thanked him profusely (as he sweated profusely) for the allowance. The next morning, Ron found his Tectocredits account had been increased by $80,000, and his appreciation for Skyler Neuwirth doubled on the spot.

On days five and six of his Denver stop, Ron e-bussed and biked to some notable sights in the city: the Republic Plaza ruins, the Denver Art Museum (covered with graffiti but still open), and Cherry Creek State Park, where the reservoir (once over 130,000 acre-feet) was now a marsh of sorts.

On day seven, Ron sated a somewhat morbid interest in the border fence a few miles south of Beltway Beds. The fence was known as the "Lowmerica Line," preventing Mexicans and other Latinos—people of any kind really—from moving north. It wasn't easy for a tourist to pass southward, either. Special permits were required from the Neo-Mexican authorities and the Upper U.S. State Department. The latter was notorious for delaying or outright denying applications, especially for anyone trying to enter the North.

South of the Lowmerica Line, whole cities stood deserted. Putrid odors emanated from crumbling buildings, where rotting corpses were not uncommon. Recently expired homeless Latinos lay stewing in heat-filled rooms; "Okies" and "Arkies" weren't rare either. The living were mostly miserable with heat, hunger, and sicknesses associated with heat and hunger. All were stuck between a rock and a hard spot: Mesoland to the south and the Lowmerica Line to the north.

Biking toward the Line, Ron already pondered the godawful reality: Without the border fence, people from the South would flood the North beyond its capacity to feed and house everyone, jeopardizing the lives of residents and migrants. He'd seen the tip of that iceberg in Seattle. Upper USA had become something of a lifeboat. If everyone "at sea" was invited onto the boat, it would surely sink as its passengers starved.

The road toward the Lowmerica Line, while not crowded, was in disrepair and eventually impassable. A mile short of the Line, Ron resorted to pushing the rental bike, and soon encountered a gruff-looking border patrol officer—Officer Gutierrez—heading back to work after several days off. Ron explained that he had been hearing a lot about the fence, and he wanted to see it. At first, Officer Gutierrez eyed Ron speculatively as though examining him for ulterior motives. Plenty of people from the Upper USA invented elaborate schemes, attempting to sneak loved ones over the border from Lowmerica. But something about Ron's candidness convinced the officer that Ron was truly curious and not conniving.

As they walked the cracked and broken road, the unlikely duo passed through a handful of miniature "cardboard communities," which were just as they sounded. Ron wondered how they survived; Officer Gutierrez muttered something about jackrabbits and prickly pear. Prior to arriving at the Line, Gutierrez explained what Ron was about to see (evidently to brace him for the sight, or maybe as a warning of what things to avoid). The barrier would be double fenced; each fence 20 feet tall, with 100 feet between them. The fences were made of sturdy wire mesh, barbed at the top, and mounted on standardized 20' posts so they could be taken down easily and moved northward when necessary.

Pit bulls and Dobermans guarded the area between the fences. Ron was astounded and couldn't help thinking that the pit bulls were for the shorter folk, with Dobermans for the tall. As if these ferocious canines weren't enough, guard towers with machine gunners were spaced to stop anyone who made it past them. Officer Gutierrez averred, "You'd have to be Tectonica Tom to get through it," in reference to the superhero of "Tectonic Terrors," a popular 3-D game.

For a fleeting moment Ron imagined Alf responding, "Tectonica Tom would get his ass chewed in the process, too." There was nothing about the Lowmerica Line that offered any hope to a northbound human, or mammal of any kind for that matter.

The more he thought about the Lowmerica Line, Ron's ambiguity was only accentuated. He was impressed by the sheer effectiveness of the Line, but he empathized with everyone south of it. He understood the need for it while lamenting the misfortune of the southerners below it. As Officer Gutierrez reached his post, AR-45 now unleashed from its shoulder holster, Ron simply said, "Thank you" and turned back toward Beltway Beds. A few seconds later, Gutierrez returned, "Adios, amigo."

Goodbye, friend. Goodbye, observer. Goodbye and a good life to you...and leave the border to me.

Plastic Plaza

Ron waited days for an eastbound train, as few people traveled that way anymore. He finally boarded the *Eastern Limited* and watched a mix of brown and green landscapes appear and fade as he escaped eastern Colorado and Nebraska. The land seemed barren for the most part, although in eastern Nebraska, small farms showed signs of life. It was June, and spelt was fairly jumping out of the soil, much like corn had jumped from the Nebraskan soil before the Wasteful.

Nebraska rolled on and on...and on. The mixed-power trains of the 22nd century were hardly super-sonic, but eventually they crossed the Missouri River. Ron missed it, asleep in the late afternoon, but missed little, as the Missouri was bone dry. He was hardly awake when they crossed the Mississippi River, too, early the next morning. Again, he didn't miss much. The Mississippi at Omaha was a concrete canal with a few feet of muddy water. "Forever Chemical" the locals called it.

Five hours later the intercom announced that the train was approaching Chicago. Once the third largest city in the USA, Chicago was one of the northernmost cities of Lowmerica and still heavily populated. Its days as an international transport hub had ended with the phenomenon of fossil fueling, but Chicago was still a center of whatever commerce and culture Lowmerica could generate. It wasn't far from Wisconsin and Milwaukee, now the heart of the Upper USA, with Wisconsin being one of the few states of relatively reliable water supplies.

Ron had read, back on Tang, that "skyscrapers" had originated in Chicago. The city's skyline was among the tallest in the world, historically and supposedly even now. Yet Ron was surprised to see, as Chicago rolled into sight, row upon row of low-rise six-story buildings, punctuated by only a handful of skyscrapers. The latter included a 110-story building called the Willis Tower (the old Sears Building), the Aon Center, the Shanshan Building, and the NRA Towers. Aside from the lower floors, these buildings were mostly empty now, but they were more or less maintained in memory of Chicago's history and, in the case of the NRA Towers, the Second Amendment ("Big Gun Money" was the more cynical reference).

Chicago was adjacent to Lake Michigan, which

was still the biggest lake—area-wise—within a single country. The lake helped moderate the city's temperature somewhat, but it was an ecological wreck in the southern reaches. It had a high bacteria count, known and unknown toxins, some truly filthy beaches, and little in the Chicago Harbor aside from Asian carp. The latter, though, managed to animate the surface, jumping to and fro like crickets in a teff field, visible only for an instant apiece, yet making quite a splash. It was as if they were all trying to escape the toxic mix of the harbor but, finding the air quality hardly better—and gravity too great a challenge—dropped quickly back to their filthy fate. The locals called them "liver challengers" because those who were desperate enough to eat them (and plenty indeed were desperate enough) were exposed to a toxic load, biomagnified in the fatty tissues of fish.

Despite the moderating effect of Lake Michigan, the city with its continental coordinates was dangerously hot in summer; hotter still from the "heat island" effect. The hard, solar-soaking surfaces of roads, sidewalks, and buildings made Chicago on average 12 degrees hotter than the surrounding rural areas; sometimes 20 degrees hotter at night. The heat island effect over such a large area also increased the frequency and intensity of thunderstorms. So, the "Windy City" was now a hot rainy city in summer, with flash flooding a frequent threat, while winters brought more ice than snow.

Buildings without cross-ventilation became unlivable in summer, so most had been torn down, abandoned, or used for storage. West of the city, nearly a hundred thousand acres of DeKalb County, soils too exhausted for agriculture now, was covered with wind and solar farms. Still, there wasn't enough electricity for air conditioning more than a few buildings, most with connections to Tang. (Rumor had it the NRA Towers even maintained thousands of square feet of cold storage below its first-floor steakhouse.)

The *Eastern Limited* eventually stopped at Union Station in the heart of the city. Gripping his backpack firmly, he hopped off amidst a noisy, jostling crowd. While he wasn't inclined to dwell on it, Ron realized that most of the people here were Black Hispanics, or Afro-Latino in more cultural terms. It was a vigorous crowd, but then you had to be, if only to stay on your feet in such a shape-shifting wave of humanity.

Though Ron was eager to explore the city, he first decided to contact the couple—Piri and Maritza Garza—that Shirley had referred him to. She'd said they were reliable and trustworthy. He didn't have to fear explaining that his family was one of the 100; he'd be welcome to talk with them freely. "They'd be among the Conveners if they were here," Shirley had insisted.

Ron took a pedicab to the Garza's house south of "Plastic Plaza," as the local park was aptly nicknamed. Ron had never seen so much plastic packed into a city block; a whole tar-sand deposit must have gone into this one, Ron speculated half seriously. All the surrounding houses were plastic as well, except of course for wiring and fittings. The Garza house was a "Plastic Classic" with the checkered roof characteristic of the region and the time.

Piri was tall and slender, with thin eyebrows and intense eyes, while Maritza was curvy, open-looking, and totally effusive. Thrilled to meet a friend of Shirley's, Maritza invited him immediately to stay with them for the duration of his Chicago visit. Without hesitating, Ron accepted the offer, delighted to avoid the hassle of locating a suitable place on his own.

Maritza showed Ron the layout, evincing a certain pride of ownership. Yet the Garza's wanted to leave Chicago and move to Wisconsin, if only they could get the permits (one apiece from the Upper USA and Wisconsin).

The Garza's took a strong interest in Ron, Tang, and the 100. Despite his lingering paranoia about Lu Ming surveilling him, Ron saw no need to keep his homeland a secret; in fact, he was slowly, almost subconsciously plotting a public information campaign of sorts. He didn't know what would come of it, but he was discomfited by the fact that almost no one had even heard of Tang.

On the other hand, he wasn't quite sure what needed to be revealed. It struck him for the first time how little he himself knew about the 100. What exactly were they trying to hide? Was it simply the gawdy wealth they enjoyed? Or was there something more nefarious behind the scenes? And was there even a concerted effort among the Tangian families to keep a low profile? Perhaps it was really Northland Security and its Tectonica overseers that kept Tang's secrets, with the 100 simply rolling along with blissful ignorance.

Piri and Maritza, like many of the better educated couples, had no children. They knew that conditions on Earth were only going to get worse before they ever got better, thanks to the economic and political decisions of the Wasteful and even since. Governments were still hellbent on "economic growth" despite the popularity enjoyed by the "Degrowth Movement" before the curriculum downsizing of 2125.

Piri and Maritza had grown up in degrowth families, and they knew the human "ecological footprint" was more than the planet could sustain. Yes, major adjustments had already occurred: the human population was down to three billion from a whopping eight billion in the Early Wasteful. Yet humans—Americans more than any others—had set into a motion some truly catastrophic processes that were literally existential threats. Well into play already was the Sixth Great Extinction, global heating, and a collection of nuclear safety issues that made the planet a casino for the human genome. Forever chemicals would be forever threatening and were still originating from numerous sectors. Soils were eroded or exhausted over huge areas, cattle were almost non-existent (especially in Lowmerica), and commercial fisheries had been relegated to small offshore stocks and massive (and massively polluting) aquaculture facilities along the Mississippi and Missouri Rivers, primarily.

Yet the crisis that kept ecologists awake at night-was the positive feedback loop between the global temperature and methane emissions. As Earth heated and permafrost melted, methane was released from its previously icy lockdown. A powerful greenhouse gas, it in turn contributed quickly and substantially to global heating. By 2145, the "ticking methane bomb" was in full explosion mode, and climate scientists (at a low ebb since the curriculum downsizing) offered a wide range of predictions for when it might stop. None of them were pleasant; some were wrenching.

That evening, as Maritza made teffcakes and pigeon eggs for the three, Ron and the Garzas talked about some of Chicago's particular problems, including nitrates and PCBs in the Chicago Harbor. Eventually, though, the topic turned to the food on the table. Food was a subject close to Maritza's heart, and there was never enough of it at the markets, she told him. The farmland surrounding the city had once been part of the world's greatest breadbasket, but the hot, wilting weather had ushered the corn, oats, and barley all the way into northern Wisconsin and primarily Canada. Wheat might have been growable—maybe—but the climate was too humid. "Most of the grain we find in Chicago is spelt and teff from South Dakota," Maritza told Ron, a tinge of worry in her tone.

Meanwhile, in the Dakotas, erosion was a huge problem. Plant diseases and pests had also multiplied with the heat and, in the eastern portions, the humidity. Fertilizers and pesticides were hard to come by, and of course the fossil-fueled farming equipment was gone, figuratively at least. (While gone figuratively, it literally littered the countryside like dinosaurs ranging in size from little Kubota tractors to the brontosaurus-sized wheat combines of the Wasteful.)

"They've been working on solutions, but I don't know..." Piri faded off, searching his mind for at least one example. He slowly lifted a forkful of teffcake toward his mouth, then suspended the fork in midair as he recalled, "One of the aquaculture companies wanted to open up Lake Oahe to a vein of salt near Pierre; then they could grow sea bream. They had a point, too, because the water's already too briny for freshwater species. The problem is, with a flood, you'd threaten the whole Missouri River down to Omaha!"

Fork still suspended, Piri added, "Well, Marit, I think we'll be having teffcake for a while yet." Maritza chuckled as Piri's fork finally hit home, and Ron made a mental note to check the location of Pierre on his Tectonica.

Later, the Garzas described some of the ways Chicagoans tried to lower the city's temperature, and the next day Ron went out to see some of these measures for himself. Sure enough, tiny gardens, miniature shrublands, and even some modest shade trees clung to life in old parking lots with sufficient cracking. A reflective but low-glare paint called "Coolseal" covered many of the roadways and bike paths. Rooftops were painted white to reflect the heat. Thankfully a few of the old city parks remained, too, including Garfield Park where Ron sought the shade of an oak tree. It was a live oak; a species that used to be found in the Gulf States of the South. Here it was alive and well in Chicago, valuable not only for shade but for seed stock.

As Ron found an unoccupied spot in the shade, his Tectonica announced, "Call from Julia." He was pleasantly surprised; she usually didn't call from work. He was really surprised when she said, "Come meet me at the station!"

"Hmmm...station? I'm in Chicago!"

"So am I," Julia explained amidst a burst of background noise. She raised her voice, "Union Station no less. I'll be waiting on the bench by Track 33, if I can find a seat. I can't believe how crowded this place is!"

Ron said, "I can't believe you're in the crowd!" Incredulous, he almost wondered if it was some kind of Lu Ming trickery, designed to root him out.

"I'm here alright. Come and get me!" It was definitely Julia, sounding happy and excited.

Ron ignored the pedicabs lining Garfield Park and located a Fastoff with a miniature nuclear engine. Fastoffs were rare and expensive, but he was eager to get to the station. The streets were almost too crowded to do justice to a Fastoff, but here and there the driver found pockets where she could jockey past the pedicabs with short bursts of speed. Within ten minutes Ron was at the station, and sure enough, Julia was directly under the Track 33 sign, suitcase in hand.

As quickly as Ron could negotiate the crowd, the two were hugging tightly. It had to be a short hug, so her suitcase wouldn't walk away, so they hugged again a second time. Ron couldn't think of anything more appropriate than, "What are you doing here?" He knew she liked him and would be happy to see him but suspected there had to be more to the story. You don't just get yourself from Anchorage to Chicago for the sake of pleasantries.

"Well, there's some stuff I have to tell you, and it had to be in person. Let's go somewhere we can talk. And eat. I haven't eaten since Minneapolis."

The two walked five blocks to a long-standing restaurant that had seen a string of proprietors from Polish to Mexican to Salvadoran to Russian, back to Polish again and now, Afro-Latino. Relieved to find a fairly quiet booth in the mid-afternoon, Julia began, "You know I like you, Ron. I wanted to see you again and didn't want to wait until you got back."

Ron had never been so grateful, yet he knew there was more to the story. Julia looked a little pale, too, as if she were afraid of something, or maybe not feeling well.

"But obviously that's not the only reason I'm here," Julia continued. "You know about COVID-39, right?" Ron averred he didn't know much, but his friend Alf had mentioned it. Unlike earlier bouts of COVID, it was more of a regional epidemic, because quarantining and vaccine development were thankfully swift and successful. Some people called it COVID-AK, as hardly anyone got it south of Alaska and the adjoining Canadian provinces.

"Yes," Julia continued, "they figured it came from a stretch of melted permafrost where some archaeologists dug up some ground-sloth remains and contracted the virus. Half the people in Alaska got it before the vaccine was ready. The problem is, the first batch of vaccine was contaminated. I'm really sick, Ron."

"What? How could they contaminate something like that?" Ron was incredulous.

"Well, I'm no chemist, but the way they described it, the vaccine had an acetic acid base that was contaminated with lithium ions. That's all I really remember about it. Then there's some other chemical reaction... lithium carbonate or something like that... and it just chews up your liver."

"From my first day working at Fantaste, I saved all I could to make a trip here, because Northwestern Memorial Hospital is the only place that's done some research on it. They're supposed to have a treatment. Technically it's still 'experimental' so they can't distribute it, but they administer it as part of the research program.

"Then, when I heard you'd be in Chicago, I knew it was the right time to make the trip."

Ron chose that moment to pull the pendant from his backpack and place it over Julia's head. "I hope this is as durable as the petrified wood from the Pacific Northwest." The meaning of "this" was vague, but each of them knew it pertained to more than the pendant.

Ron didn't want to take advantage of the Garza's hospitality but wondered if there was some way Julia could stay at their place with him. Julia could go to a hotel, of course, but he'd like to have as much time with her as possible. There was only one way to find out; he grabbed her suitcase and told her to follow him.

They arrived at the Garza home just as Maritza was returning from her shift at the M&M factory. Chicago had once been the "candy capital" of the world, and there was still a lot of candy-making done in the city; another vice that helped people through hard times.

"Hi Ron. Who do we have here?" Maritza inquired before she was even completely off her bike.

"Maritza, this is Julia. We met in Anchorage. She's come to Chicago for some medical treatments, and I was hoping you could recommend a hotel for her," Ron said, hoping Maritza would invite Julia to stay instead.

Sure enough, she did.

"Don't be silly. We've got room here. Julia, we would love to have you stay with us. Please, make yourself at home."

After Julia unpacked in one of the guest rooms, it was time for dinner. Maritza brought out some spelt chips and salsa. Once considered an appetizer, spelt chips and salsa had become a traditional main course. Tomatoes and chilis were still plentiful; onions were mostly shipped down from Wisconsin. On occasion, the Garzas splurged and bought corn chips, too, as Black Aztec varieties were still hand-gardened in the region.

Julia needed to be at the hospital the next morning. It was a long walk from the Plastic Plaza district, so Ron accompanied her the whole way. By the time they reached the Toxins Center and got Julia checked in, it was nearly 10:00. Ron waited in the lobby and read about the history of Chicago on his Tectonica until she was finally finished at noon.

"They want me to come back every day for the next three weeks for chelation treatments. They think they can reduce the lithium levels to a safe amount for my liver." Julia sounded hopeful. "Oh Ron, I know you probably don't want to stay in Chicago for that long. I wouldn't either. Maybe we could hang out here for a few days, and then you could do the rest of your journey and come back here at the end of my treatments. What do you think?"

Ron was encouraged by the news and liked the plan Julia proposed. "Let's do it!" he confirmed and asked if she had anything she wanted to see in Chicago. "The Art Institute!" Julia blurted. "It's world famous and they have some classic paintings like 'American Gothic' and 'Nighthawks.'" Ron knew little about art, but Julia's enthusiasm was infectious, and there was no way he'd discourage her with a "no."

They hailed a pedicab to the museum and spent most of the afternoon perusing the art, catching glimpses of each other, and occasionally holding hands. Now and then, Julia got weak and slightly nauseous; they'd find a bench and sit it out.

After her second treatment the next morning, they went on an architectural tour, floating down the Chicago River in a mule-powered paddleboat, while a guide pointed out at least 20 styles of building in the city. Most of the taller buildings—except in the financial center—were now unoccupied beyond the first five floors, but the pair found it interesting to learn of the nuanced architectural differences they'd never thought of.

On the third afternoon, they followed a map they bought at a local market to "Gangland Chicago," and visited places where infamous events like the Valentine's Day Massacre and the Leopold and Loeb killing had taken place. Oddly, these places seemed almost quaint, as mass killings with ARs of several generations (AR-15s, AR-33s, and AR-45s especially) had turned Chicago into the "Mass Murder Capitol of the World." Not that city leaders embraced the title; it was bestowed upon them by a video of the same name, and the media ran with it. It was certainly fitting, though, with over 30,000 gun-related homicides—mostly in mass killings—since the video came out in 2025.

Ron was astounded that, despite Chicago's grizzly nickname, the NRA Towers still stood tall and proud. He'd heard the story, though. An economist named Becker had developed the argument that the best answer for more gun violence was actually (and unbelievably) more guns! The "gun violence Kuznets curve," he called it. He said it was a close call—the cost:benefit assessment was complicated—but opting for the more-guns approach gave a significant boost to GDP (gun sales, ammunition, medical bills, etc.). That had put it over the political top, such that no Congress was ever able to ban ARs. The horse was so far out of the barn now, no one seriously tried to rope it back in.

On the fourth day since Julia's arrival, and after dozens of reassuring hugs and kisses, Ron continued on to the next destination and left Julia in the trusted hands of the Garzas and the capable doctors of Northwestern Memorial. The sooner he completed his fact-finding tour, the sooner he could return to Julia. He didn't plan on ever leaving her again for such a length of time.

At the Margin

Ron's destination was New York City, the intellectual heart of the country according to some. He boarded the train, found a window seat, and found his thoughts divided among Julia, New York, and the train. He could have traveled on the high-speed train, the *Big Apple Express*. It was the only high-speed train in the USA, Upper or Lower. But Ron stayed with the *Eastern Limited*—every bit as limited as eastern—because he wanted to see the country. He didn't realize it would be horribly off schedule half the time for reasons ranging from breakdowns to supply chain issues to freight train rights-of-way. The rail line, SoTrak, was notorious for delays, especially on the *Limited*, and everyone called it "SloTrak."

As the *Limited* managed to slow-track itself out

of Illinois and into Upper American Indiana, Ohio, and Pennsylvania, Ron witnessed a tapestry of spelt fields, chicken coops, truck farms, cabins, and small orchards of fig and dragon fruit. The most extensive "ecosystems," of sorts, were the mind-numbing mudflats along Lake Erie and the rolling thickets of kudzu-covered mimosas in Pennsylvania. Shanty towns and line camps were fairly everywhere, and now and then the *Limited* rolled into old-fashioned, quainter towns with church steeples and courthouses. After three days of Upper Americana, the *Limited* was finally in New Jersey, and quickly to the shore, as New Jersey was only about 50 miles across now, given the receding Eastern Shore.

One city had managed to migrate from its Wasteful Century base all the way into the 22nd century, moving west with the shore, toppling over the smaller, weaker towns of the old Pine Barrens. The evidence of this process was seen on a billboard near the shore:

EXPERIENCE ATLANTIC CITY——THE NEW VENICE!

Like the old Venice in Italy, prior to its final submergence in the late Wasteful, much of what remained of Atlantic City was supported on plastic pylons and platforms. Otherwise, it hadn't changed much! There were casinos and restaurants and hotels, all constructed on the plastic above sea level. And, as another billboard mawkishly displayed, gondolas were used for transporting gamblers and tourists from one joint to the next. One gondola service run by Italian Americans claimed it was using oars "passed down from ancient Venice."

As tempting as a gondola ride might seem, Ron stayed on the *Limited.* He couldn't see everything, and the focus of this leg of the journey was New York. Besides, gondola services were operating there as well. In fact, a passenger explained to Ron that the whole bottom half of Manhattan, after billion-dollar programs to stave off the inevitable, had finally surrendered to "The Pond." Lower Manhattan had been built on landfill—most of it less than 15' above sea level—and proved impossible to fortify against the irrepressible sea. After one final, futile attempt to build a seawall strong enough to protect all of Manhattan, the whole financial district—Wall Street and all—was "moved" to Upper Manhattan, meaning mainly that the e-banks and e-brokers took new zip codes north of Central Park.

Fortunately, Grand Central Terminal was still on solid footing; still well over 100' above sea level. And it was still one of the busiest train stations in the Western Hemisphere. But other parts of the metropolitan area—a good portion of Brooklyn, Queens, and the Rockaways—had been evacuated and abandoned to the rising waters.

When Ron climbed off the train at Grand Central,

he could hardly believe his eyes. People of every imaginable race, age, and manner of dress were moving around in every direction—fast! Overwhelmed by it all, he realized that he hadn't given enough thought as to where he might stay, or even to what he might do in the city.

He stopped at a high-priced coffee shop—they sold real coffee and not just coppee—and rang Megan for help. Ron was halfway through a "Big Apple Cappuccino" when Megan returned the call and gave him the name and address of someone who might be able to help. His name was Dr. James Kettering, a former classmate of hers from Rutgers and a tenured professor of economics at Columbia University. Columbia had survived curriculum downsizing because of its fame and powerful alumni. (Ron seemed to recall that a few of the 100 had even attended Columbia.) Ron thanked Megan profusely, capped off his cappuccino, and called Kettering.

"Kettering here," a somewhat clipped voice responded. Ron introduced himself, referenced Megan, and explained his situation.

Kettering paused for a pregnant moment as Ron glanced anxiously at the Tectonica's battery level. "Well," Kettering finally allowed, "I'm semi-retired, and we do happen to be on summer break right now." Another, briefer pause followed, and finally Kettering obliged, "A friend of Megan is a friend of mine. I'd be pleased to put you up and show you around a little. I should revisit a few places myself!"

Kettering gave directions to his apartment in Brooklyn, and Ron repeated them to the first pedicab driver he could hail. The cabbie hustled them to the ferry that took them over New Brooklyn Bay (Brooklyn wasn't new, but most of the bay was post-Wasteful), off the other side, and up to Bay Ridge, where Ron got out at an old brick building with rusty fire escapes. Ron's first thought was, "Not plastic?!" He climbed the cement steps and rang an old-fashioned bell for apartment 2B. Dr. Kettering buzzed him in, and Ron climbed a musty stairway to the second floor and the 2B door.

"Come in, come in. And tell me a little about Tang. I'm an economist, after all, and it seems I've been missing a big part of the economic picture."

Ron thought, "That was fast!" but found himself just as eager to talk about Tang as Kettering. He wondered who would learn more from the discussion and mentioned as much. Kettering chuckled, "I'll learn more from your thoughts, and you'll learn more from mine."

Ron kept a fleeting thought to himself, "That sounds economic."

A couple hours and cold beers later, Kettering scratched his chin. "So, this is the place pulling the strings. Running big business and the big cities too." Kettering suddenly punctuated his succinct observation with a yell, "Worldwide!"

Washing down the thought with a quick gulp of beer, Kettering elaborated, "You know, Ron, I sensed something like that was going on, because even the directors and officers never seem to make a final call on anything. I remember wondering once, when Columbia had a big research proposal on the table, 'Who's got *them* by the balls?' Even the CEO said he'd have to make a call first. His Tectonica was probably satellinked on a one-bounce to Tang!"

Ron said, "Yeah, I suppose, although I don't know anything about Tectonica and satellites."

"Neither do I," Kettering said with a grin. "I just made that up."

Ron found Kettering easy to like. The professor obviously knew a lot about the world but wasn't arrogant about it. He was easy to talk with and, despite the heaviness of the topics, a humorous fellow besides. He reminded Ron of Alf, albeit a more intellectual version.

Now it was Kettering's turn to regale Ron with stories of New York. He'd minored in history at Rutgers, so his stories were spiced with historical flair. "New York was the biggest city in the USA from 1760 on, and still is, even after the Plunges." The steep declines in population and GDP toward the end of the Wasteful Century were called "the Plunges" by economists. Kettering continued, "It was long known as the cultural, financial, and media capital of the world, and that's also still true. The headquarters of many international corporations are still here, as well as the stock exchange. New York also has a strong high-tech development industry called Silicon Alley."

"It sure has every kind of people," Ron said, referencing the variegated mass of humanity he'd seen at Grand Central Terminal.

"Yes, New York was the original 'melting pot,' as they called it; the gateway to America, and we've taken immigrants from every country in the world. On the other hand, most immigration hasn't been allowed since 2076, when the No New New Yorkers Act was passed. What you saw at the train station is the result of many decades, three centuries really, of immigration from before 2076, plus a disintegration of Americana. By 2076, immigrant communities were mostly settling into their own territories, speaking their own languages, cooking their own foods and the like. 800 languages are spoken in New York. The Statue of Liberty—Lady Liberty, we call her—would be very proud, but maybe a little confused, too.

"So, in some ways, New York today is like it was in the 19th century: a collection of immigrant communities mixed into a more-or-less 'American' matrix. It's a matrix of markets, democracy, municipality, and courts. It kind of works, but it's hardly a well-oiled machine. Unfortunately, we have gangs galore, too, and some of them are armed to the teeth. God damn the NRA!

"Global heating really changed things, too. Obviously, I wasn't around before it started, but it's been going on my whole life, with no signs of stopping. As an economist, I can't blame people for the high discount rates they seem to gamble with. The future looks about as certain as a shooting star sometimes!

"Anyway, we've seen drastic changes in the transportation sector. You saw New Brooklyn Bay; took the New Brooklyn Bay Ferry. There was no ferry when I was a child because there was no New Brooklyn Bay. We've got three other ferries in the metropolitan area that weren't here a hundred years ago. I guess the ferry operators are happy, at least.

"Not so with most of the sectors, though. We once had the busiest airspace in North America. Now it's mostly limited to the private jets of the super-rich—maybe some from Tang—which land on the Central Park Runways. We had two huge airports, LaGuardia and JFK, that flooded out during the Wasteful.

"New York also had the largest bus fleet in the world. Now we've got an electric streetcar line with about three percent the old bus-line capacity. When cars were outlawed, we had some room for the tracks. The problem is, the streetcar lines run on solar and wind, and as you know (although Ron didn't), battery storage has been the downfall of renewably powered transportation. It's not like we have continuous sunlight or wind here, plus with all the gangs it's been nearly impossible to maintain large arrays of solar and wind facilities.

"The subway system is still in use, but of course a lot of the trains had to be re-routed aboveground. In fact, most routes never even go underground now; some smart alecks even call it the "Misnomerway." It works okay, I'd say. Subway electricity comes mostly from tidal-powered generators along the coast, and those are a lot harder for the gangs to pillage.

"The Port of New York and New Jersey, about thirty miles north," Kettering lifted his beer to indicate the direction," still handles a fair amount of cargo. It's all by sailing ships and barges now.

"You know, Ron, New York City was described as 'hot' in the summertime 200 years ago, but that must have been a picnic compared to today. We have eight times the number of days over 100 degrees than they had at the beginning of the Wasteful. The heat-island effect is really pronounced here, and all the tall build-ings block the wind. They make little microclimates—breezes here and there—but anything resembling a cooler air mass tends to get pushed up over the skyline and turns into a thunderhead!

"New York finally started using more reflective, lighter-colored materials for buildings and roadways, like they've done in Chicago, and trees were planted among the street cracks. You'll find some rooftop gar-dens here and there, too. Still, we lose three or four thousand people every summer to heatstroke, and of course they're almost all kids, the elderly, or people with respiratory or heart ailments. The rich have air conditioning, but most of the city suffers when the heat goes up. We've tried to provide public cooling centers for the most afflicted, but not everyone can manage to make it there in time. There isn't always room to accommodate everyone, either."

Kettering took a longer-than-usual pause, culminating in a deep breath, and concluded philosophically, "Ron, a lot of us old-time New Yorkers are still proud of this city, for what it was if not for what it is. But you know, a city is always partly what it was, and New York had so much that 'partly' is still a lot. So, tomorrow we'll take a tour, and you can see for yourself. Meanwhile, you can take the guest room," which Ron gladly did, sleeping more in one night than he had in three on the *Limited*.

The next morning, after a coffee-coppee mix in Kettering's kitchenette, Ron asked, "Dr. Kettering..."

Kettering cut him off and commanded, "Call me Jim!"

"Jim, I can't tell you how grateful I am for the hospitality. And I can't wait to see the city! Where're we headed first?"

"First is Fifth, but who's on Second?" Jim quipped, quoting another New York duo that never quite died. Ron looked utterly confused, so Jim added, "I'll tell you about Abbott and Costello a little later."

No sooner had they dropped down from Bay Ridge with Kettering's favorite pedicabby—improbably named Alfie—than they were shuttling through blocks of utter poverty, only to emerge again in smaller areas of affluence. Invariably the latter were gated and usually on higher ground, with armed guards, robots and drones pitching in on security. One area had a sign that succinctly warned, "Cameras, Guard Dogs, Electric Fences."

Alfie dropped them off at the southeast corner of Central Park, and they walked along 57th Street to Fifth Avenue. Before the Wasteful, fashionable shops would have run for miles to the south; Millionaire's Row to the north. Now it was somewhat of a crapshoot to the south, and Billionaire's Row to the north. The crapshoot could be dangerous at night, but during the day it could be interesting and entertaining. Certainly, some of the better dining options remained along Fifth; pizza was as prevalent as ever. For that matter, some of the shops remained as well; shoes and clothing shops especially, plus souvenir shops, jewelry stores, a few video stores, and three Tectonica outlets. Ron and Jim would walk it all the way down to Washington Square, where Alfie would pick them up after dinner.

Many of the shops on Fifth had their own armed guards, and New York City police were seldom out of sight. The police were armed primarily with AR-45s, and some had dogs; bicycle cops carried only hand-guns. Although the presence of so much firepower made Ron uncomfortable, that discomfort was approximately balanced by reassurances of high-powered public safety. When Ron heard a couple of shots toward late morning, only blocks away, Jim said, "24th Street as usual. But don't worry; that area is crawling with..." Before he could finish the sentence, six shots rang out; much louder shots in a decisive sequence. "Cops," Jim finished his sentence.

Jim and Ron decided to stop for a slice of pizza while the police finished up with the 24th St. incident. The goat-cheese, tomato-and-basil pizza at Parsa's Pies did the city justice, thin teff crust and all. Next to Parsa's was a jewelry store, and Ron bought Julia a pair of earrings, supposedly of pearl from Sandy Hook Bay. Real or fake, they were beautiful and would hold special significance for Julia.

The day went on, with Ron and Jim exploring the sights, scenes, and a handful of shops along Fifth, finally reaching Washington Park around 5:00 p.m. While it was mostly a day of tourism, for Ron it also an education, as Jim—Dr. Kettering no less—continued with lessons of history, economics, geography, and New York society. One thing stuck with Ron more than the rest. Dr. Kettering had opined, "They taught us in economics courses that the Plunges were the worst episodes in modern economic history. The thing is, they invariably used a plunging GDP and stock market to prove their point, and eventually it struck me they were wagging the dog with the tail. I mean, of course GDP and the market would shrink in a context of COVID pandemics, water shortages, pollution problems, the end of Big Oil, and global heating! You didn't have to be an ecologist to figure that out. Yet they acted like GDP was the measure of success, instead of a red flag for how much human activity the planet could take.

"Well Ron, I teach the kids differently in my courses. I suppose those puppeteers up on Tang wouldn't like it, but hopefully my tenure at Columbia is good for something. If they're still trying to milk more money out of our poor little planet, I think they're borderline criminal. Nothing against your father, Ron—probably half the 100 don't realize what things are like around the world—but I wish they all were sent down to Mesoland for a week!"

These were strong words, yet Ron realized that Kettering made more sense than any economics lesson he'd had on Tang. He was right: GDP was everything there, and stock market reports were the default on most Tectonica displays, on and off Tang. It seemed wrong-headed and, based on what Ron had seen thus far in his travels, dangerous. The USA and the world, really, needed to back off the push for GDP and push instead for a healthier planet and a better deal for the masses of poor people.

Jim spotted Alfie's pedicab circling Washington Park, so they flagged him down, hungry and thinking about dinner. Before they reached the cab, though, they heard music ringing out from a few streets away. Jim said, "That must be the Italian Pride Festival... I saw it scheduled on the Tectonica. That might be interesting yet. Some of Little Italy drowned with Lower Manhattan, but most of it's still there and the festival might actually be a good place for dinner." Alfie pulled up, and they drove the ten blocks to the festival area.

As they approached the barricaded streets, banners and Italian flags waved on every side, and horse-drawn carts pulled floats depicting the glories of bel paese. An animated group of young men and women in rustic costumes performed a traditional tarantella on a stage, sweat soaking their clothes and streaming down their faces. Ron and Jim got out at a concession cart, with Jim lamenting that Italian sausage just wasn't the same made from soy, but "good enough" at the end of a long day. The sausage was definitely good enough, Ron thought, although the afternoon was too hot to fully enjoy any kind of food outdoors. They ate their sausage sandwiches in the partial shade of a huge Russian olive tree, which Ron recognized as the "bane bush" of Anchorage. It was no bane here, though. As hungry as Ron was, the shade was even more welcome than the soy. The shade was partial due only to the fact that a (mostly Italian) crowd had assembled in it, so Ron and Jim found only the edge of it available. The crowding was unfortunate because there was no way not to notice the body odor—Italian or otherwise—wafting over and sometimes superseding the scent of the soy sausages. All in all, the dinner was similar to the shade: partially fulfilling.

Ron slept like a rock again that night in Kettering's guest room, and the next day was similar to the first, but with further-flung destinations that kept Alfie busier. First, they went to the Empire State Building, for many years the tallest building in the world and a quintessential symbol of the city. By 2145, with many other skyscrapers out of commission or even gone, the Empire stood out almost like it had in the early 20th century and could be seen for miles. It was surprisingly well-maintained, and they could actually take an elevator to the top for an incredible view of the city and beyond. "It's the highest functioning elevator in the USA now," Jim noted, and Ron appreciated.

Next, Alfie brought them to an electric water taxi with a glass bottom that brought tourists over the sunken World Trade Towers Memorial. Given the origins of the memorial, plus the fact that the memorial itself had originally centered on the highest artificial waterfall in the world, the glass-bottom tour was perhaps the most surreal experience Ron would ever have.

They made a quick foray into Central Park, entering from the west side. For a parcel of land valued at $528 billion in the early 21st century, thanks to a visionary landscape design by Frederick Law Olmsted, the park was now a sad sight. The monuments and buildings were vandalized and plastered with graffiti, while the greenspace was mostly brown with wear, littered, and filled with homeless camps. Each morning, horse-drawn wagons passed through, collecting corpses.

They hastened back out of the park and across the street to an impressive building of brick and stonework. Here, Dr. Kettering introduced Ron to some friends of his, Brandon Kitowski and his wife Norma Kanazawa. Brandon was also a professor at Columbia, where he taught cultural anthropology (which would have been banned if the 100 knew about it). Brandon's wife was an actor on Broadway and smaller venues about the city. The couple was child-free, even though couples were allowed one child. As with the Garzas, this was a conscious decision on their part, for they knew the Earth was teetering on the brink of sustainability for humans.

Over coppee in the apartment, the foursome traded thoughts on issues that concerned them. "There were once more than 120 colleges and universities in New York," Brandon said, "and now we are down to six. Aside from Columbia, they're just glorified technical schools. It's much the same upstate, with a few exceptions up past the Adirondacks. Of course, none of the schools have cut back on business courses! Business, advertising, public relations... mostly for corporation jobs.

"A lot of the universities train students for government jobs, too, which got a lot more popular when the capital was moved from Washington, DC to Madison. That was in 2064 and it was long overdue, too. DC must have been miserable with all the heat, flooding, and just oppressive humidity. Congress couldn't manage to act on anything, but they sure acted on that! No one wanted to be in DC, so off to Wisconsin they went."

Jim's historical bent kicked in and he added, "Moving some national monuments was another thing they acted upon. Remember when they used a whole train route for a month for the Washington Monument?" Ron imagined the monument, swaddled in padding, limping along on the *Eastern Limited* or a SloTrak relative.

After the coppee and some freshening up, Norma invited the two guests to a play on 60th Street. Vaguely familiar with the glamor of New York's theater district, Ron was all for it. However, the 60th Street venue turned out to be anything but glamorous, and surprisingly small. All of 16 people were in attendance—only twice as many as the cast—and when a faded cotton curtain was raised, an intense drama unfolded. *At the Margin* amounted to a brutal critique of the lives and interests of the rich (two actors playing four characters), contrasting their affluence with the squalor and misery of the have-nots (six actors; numerous characters) living in heat and desperation. Ron was impressed that a cast of only eight could manage to deliver such a powerful social critique. Not that they posited a political solution—no Magna Carta on stage—but Ron could see how a production like this could set the stage for some serious reckoning. If his father could see him now...worse yet if Lu Ming could see him...

Norma interrupted his troubled thoughts, "I hope you liked the production, Ron. This little theatre is part of the Eastern Underground. We do social commentary, and we're careful who sees it. Our little audience this evening was hand-picked, or at least that's what we shoot for. Once in a while others find us, and we don't turn them away. We can't, really; it's not like we have a security force on staff. In fact, this evening we spotted a man in the back that none of us recognized. He was barely visible and disappeared before the final act."

"Really? What did he look like?" Ron queried with wide-open eyes and a quick glance-about.

"He seemed...indescribable somehow. Almost like he was dressed for a play himself, and not for a colorful role, either. He was in the shadow near that corner exit," Norma pointed, "and he looked kind of short and stocky. That's about all I could make out."

Ron was worried now, more than ever. *At the Margin* was a real swipe at the 100, even if it was only a proverbial swipe at a suspected 100 they knew next to nothing about. Frankly, the play bore an uncanny resemblance to the luxurious life on Tang (at least for the 100) versus the dangerous drudgery off Tang.

Ron suspected there was much more to the Eastern Underground than plays on 60th Street, too. Unlike the previous evenings at Kettering's place, his night in the guest room was disturbing. When Jim casually asked him the next morning, "How did you sleep?" Ron rubbed an eye and mumbled, "At the margin."

Wind Gods Plateau

Ron finally decided to share his concern about Lu Ming with Jim, a discerning confidant who would surely have some wise advice. After a lengthy discussion about Ron's circumstances—his journey, Julia, Lu Ming—they agreed the best course of action would be for Ron to cut his New York visit short and head to the South forthwith. His chances of shaking Lu Ming would be better there for sure. Then, assuming he came out of it alive, Ron could return to Julia in Chicago and get quickly en route to Seattle, Anchorage, and Tang.

That very day, after gathering a few supplies and calling Julia with Jim's Tectonica, Ron set out once again for Grand Central Terminal with Alfie the reliable pedicabby. Along the way they passed the Museum of Natural History, which Ron regretted missing his chance to explore. They passed the great hall and Alfie pointed to a couple of newer buildings. "Those are the Extinction Annexes. They've got bones and DNA banks and some taxidermy from the more recent extinctions. I saw the cats display with Dr. Kettering once; they had everything from bobcats to cheetahs to tigers...species from all over the world."

"That must have been depressing," Ron mulled. Alfie didn't reply; some things went without saying.

The other sight Ron regretted missing was the Statue of Liberty. Located on a small island in New York Harbor, it had been jacked up four times since 2059, as New Yorkers refused to relegate it to the rising seas. By now, the island was a distant memory, but the massively girded pedestal, made of the most durable plastic available, was something of an island itself. Ron knew about it because he knew the Swinton family from Tang, which monopolized the plastics industry via Swinton Plastics. Thanks to a relentless advertising campaign, the site was now known as much for the "Swinton Platform" as it was for Lady Liberty herself. Swinton family hubris aside, the statue was (thus far) a symbol of human determination in the face of global heating and sea-level rise, as well as a PR miracle for plastic.

When they reached Grand Central Terminal, they sat in the pedicab for ten minutes looking for any sign of a spy—Ming or potentially an assistant—who might be looking back at them. To their untrained eyes, at least, no such person came to light, so Ron bid fare-well to Alfie with a heartfelt elbow bump. He'd come to know Alfie almost as much as he'd known Alf from Anchorage. He liked them both and thought he might name a boy Alfie and call him Alf for short, should he (and Julia!) ever have a boy.

Quickly now, Ron got his mind into here-and-now mode, made his way to the Tectonica T-Ticket kiosk, and T-bought a ticket to Louisville, Kentucky. He had just enough time for a cup of coppee and a stop in the One Room (public restrooms were divided by func-tion, not gender) before boarding.

The *Southern Special* was famous to those in the railway industry, infamous to frequent riders, and largely unknown to Upper Americans. In terms of reli-ability, it made the *Eastern Limited* seem like Old Faith-ful, although the two trains were capable of similar speeds. The first thing Ron noticed about the *Special* was the not-so-special smell. The train was an olfacto-ry smorgasbord of unwanted selections: Body odor(s), Two-Room sewage, and chemically heavy soy burgers could each be detected, sometimes all at once! Thank-fully, the nose could readily forget most of these odors after a certain period of exposure, although the chemi-cal smells were noticeably durable.

The smells were exacerbated by the heat. SoTrak tried to air-condition the cars, but the one chemical needed for A/C was always the one in shortest supply. Those in the know were not surprised, because the chemical was engineered for poor storage and therefore continual sales. Despite its poor performance, "Coldon" was a winner by law, as all other coolants had been prohibited, not so much for purposes of environmental protection, but for the obscene profiting of the Caldor family from Tang.

Conductors on the *Southern Special* faced an everyday decision: Open the windows to the super-heated, humid air of the South, or keep them closed while the Coldon supply threatened to peter out in the southernmost reaches.

The southernmost reach, Ron saw from the route map above the windows, was the ominous-sounding Mesoland Containment Corridor. Ron thought, "Jesus Cristo," after an expression—Mexican he assumed— he'd heard an exasperated Officer Gutierrez mutter (waiting at length outside an occupied Two-Room short of the border). Ron was determined to take the *Special* as far south as it went, so he'd have the story of a lifetime to bring back to Tang, but he was starting to wonder if the story was worth the...whatever he was in for.

The first day of the ride was much like his three days between Illinois and New Jersey, with non-stop patchworks of small operations: small farms, small woodlots, small towns. As nighttime approached, though, so did West Virginia, and things got bigger; bigger woodlots especially, and outright forests in some areas. These were mostly eucalyptus forests, with seedstock originally from Australia. Given its convoluted topography, West Virginia had more climatological diversity, and eucalyptus did quite well along the hot, somewhat drier (less humid at least) southwestern-facing slopes. Most other areas, though, were absolutely inundated and dominated by kudzu, so much so that the underlying trees and shrubs were unidentifiable and seemingly irrelevant.

Also large—strikingly large—were the cactus-covered flats where coal corporations had scalped the mountains in the middle of the state. Ron was no ecologist, but even to him it was a surreal contrast between the densely wooded or kudzu-covered slopes and the plateaus of prickly pear and cholla. The mountaintop mining of the Wasteful had left these plateaus with scarified, infertile soils exposed to the deadly heat of the 22nd century sun, and Mother Nature was lucky if even her cacti would grow. The prickly pear and cholla ("annoya" the locals called it, as it readily latched onto anyone careless) were stunted and the palest of green in color, but the pear, at least, had some nutritional value to the bands of wild hogs roaming these flats, which in turn were prized by the "flat-hillbillies" eking out a living in these parts.

Around sunset, they topped onto a plateau with

wind turbines as far as the eye could see, and the train immediately shook and rocked as it rattled and rolled. The conductor made his last announcement of the evening: They'd reached Wind Gods Plateau (the mine-given name) at the top of West Virginia. Crew hands came through the coach cars, cracking windows slightly to take advantage of the clearer, cooler air without blowing away any customers' toupees. Ron had the fleeting thought that the Caldors would be losing a few T-debits up here (although the stored Coldon would still be dissipating at its slower, engineered rate).

It seemed like Wind Gods Plateau would go on forever, but in actuality it was four minutes until the wind turbines gave way to more eucalyptus trees. Before dozing off into a fitful, coach-class sleep, Ron had seen enough of West Virginia to impress him yet more deeply with the magnitude of human impact on Planet Earth. He remembered Jim Kettering cursing about "those damned Chicago-school economists and their GDP." With the carnage he'd seen out the window, Ron concluded West Virginia must have been the "Mother of GDP" back in the Wasteful. It was an ironic notion, what with the legacy of West Virginia poverty, yet Ron was right in a way, as coal had *fueled* a major share of economic activity for the two centuries prior to his.

Ron slept through the rest of West Virginia, slumbered through Ohio, and woke up fully in the mid-morning of a sunny Kentucky day. The Coldon

supply must have run low, and he was sweating profusely (as was, to his chagrin, the passenger quite next
to him). Ron immediately went to the dining car for a
hundred-dollar bottle of water and a SoTrak Soy Stick
and sat on one of the benches arranged like rowing
seats in a medieval slave ship. He gulped the entire
bottle of water and had a few bits of the chemically
laden stick.

Suddenly concerned about Julia, he called her,
and suddenly Julia was concerned about him. "Do you
really have to do this?" she asked. "I'm curious about
the South too, but who knows how bad it might get
down there. What if the train breaks down in a heat
spell? What if you run into bandits? Promise me you'll
stick to the train as much as possible, okay?"

Ron didn't tell her about the Mesoland Containment Corridor, and she still didn't know much about
his Lu Ming problem. He left it at, "Well, I won't have
much of a chance to look around, anyway." He quickly
changed the subject to her treatments. "Tell me how
you're doing, honey!" He had plenty of T-tokens so he
switched the Tectonica to video and selected pay-all
mode (so Julia wouldn't be charged). It was worth it to
see her beautiful face. She looked slightly thinner—a
fact she confirmed—but otherwise looked vibrant. The
treatments were going well, the doctors had told her,
and both of them were encouraged.

Suddenly Ron blurted "Gotta go, mmmmaw,"

hoping it sounded like a kiss and not a reaction to the soy stick, because in actuality it was both. Ron managed to make it to the Two-Room and to thank his lucky stars it wasn't occupied. "No more soy sticks on this trip," he declared in a whisper. Luckily there were other options, laden with different chemicals.

Done with that inconvenience, Ron decided to just text Julia back for the time being, if only to assuage her concerns about the abrupt sign-off. He told her it was all about the soy stick—no bandits or heat stroke—and she sent back a particularly relevant happy face from the millions available on a Tectonica.

The *Southern Special* made a stop in Louisville, an old river city rich in history and still the largest city in Kentucky, according to the sweat-drenched man next to Ron. It was a prominent destination from day one because the Falls of the Ohio was a natural stopping point for river navigators, and therefore the various suppliers and service providers who catered to them. Eventually it became the site of attractions like Churchill Downs, the Louisville Slugger Museum, and the Muhammad Ali Center. A few of these attractions remained in the 22nd century, plus a franchise of the NRA Museum for Gun Connoisseurs (which was really more of a gun shop selling plastic guns of sundry make and model.)

As the train and the time rolled on, it came out that the sweaty fellow next to Ron was a retired mining engineer named Levi. "Back in the eastern part of the state, we strip-mined almost three million acres of coal going back to the Wasteful," he said with a vacant stare out Ron's window. It wasn't entirely clear if he was lamenting the environmental damages or his retirement. Ron replied vaguely, "I saw a lot of that back in West Virginia."

"Yeah," Levi continued, "It played hell on the land. What you don't see from the train is all the underground mining we did, too. There's places over by Morehead and Stanton where there's more going on underground than over. I mean there's whole towns of poor folks living there now, down in the shafts and the stopes. I even heard of one guy holed up in a sump—talk about flooding risk! Most of those old mines got enough methane for the Fourth of July, too. That's why most of them boys down there chew tobacco instead of smoke."

The thought of living in a sump got even worse with the thought of chewing tobacco. "What do they do for lighting?"

"That part's dangerous, too, but most of 'em are stealin' off the grid. There's cables all around there coming from the wind farms. Them ol' boys get wire from the old power lines—it used to be all over—and they plug right in!"

"Pretty dangerous, is it?"

"Well in the mine, with all that methane, you

better be careful with the wiring. One short and it's goodnight Eilish. And then up in the grid you got power-company dogs with short fuses. Pick your poison."

"I think I'll just stay above ground."

"Well," a sweating Levi offered philosophically, "that's what we all aim to do."

Mesoland Containment Corridor

At the Bowling Green station, the *Southern Special* needed supplies and maintenance, so she was down from late in the afternoon until noon the next day. Some passengers stayed aboard, as they had nowhere else to go, but those with enough T-credits stayed elsewhere in town or, ideally, to the west of town where the air wasn't quite as hot and polluted. The stop gave Ron some time to think about the remainder of his southward tilt. The next few days would be crucial to his education; he'd probably never be this far south again.

Bowling Green was only three stops removed from the Mesoland Containment Corridor, which ran roughly along the southern boundary of Tennessee. Ron had already decided to cut his trip short of the corridor, though, for three good reasons he'd absorbed from crew and passengers alike. First, it would be unbearably hot there. Nighttime temperatures seldom dropped below 90 degrees; 120-degree days were common all summer. Second, there was nothing around the "MCC Station" except the dense infrastructure of the mile-wide corridor itself (including a three-ply fence and a matrix of traps) and a research station operated by the Mesoland Agency of the U.S. Geological Survey. Third, and quite related to the second reason, the corridor was dangerous as hell. Among other things, huge pythons were often seen just inside the high-voltage woven-wire fence along the northern boundary. Misadventurous tourists had been killed by both (pythons and the fence itself, simultaneously in a few cases).

"You'd have to be a genuine idiot to get off at the MCC," Levi had drawled with an emphasis on the "ine" in "genuine." This from a fellow who'd clearly experienced idiocy at several levels. Ron wanted no part of idiocy if he could avoid it; genuine or otherwise.

On the other hand, Ron had a streak of stubbornness to go with his curiosity and venturous spirit, and found himself wondering, "Could it really be that bad?" Luckily for him, he stumbled into some answers sooner than he could have hoped. He'd strolled over to the 1907 Tavern, a place as ancient as it sounded. It struck Ron immediately that not a single plastic item could be seen in the tavern; it was all stone, wood, iron, or brick. The place was dimly lit, and the temperature was fairly pleasant; perhaps 83 degrees. In one corner was an animated old-timer playing a harmonica for all he was worth. The ambiance—plus a long bar with a half dozen beer taps—explained why the tavern managed to stay open. The broader context—hot South and economic hardship—explained why it wasn't packed.

Ron glanced at the layout, the bar, and the heavy wooden tables, and honed in on a small group of uniformed personnel along one of the walls, drinking beer and deep in discussion. Curious, he walked past the group and, at the last second, spotted a Mesoland Agency patch on the shoulder of a young, strong-looking lady next to the aisle. The table beyond was empty, but Ron stopped, backed up a step and said, "Excuse me, but I'm not from around here and I noticed you're with the government. My train is down for the night and I'm trying to plan the rest of my trip. Would you mind if I joined you and maybe get a few tips?"

"We only tip the bartender!" the oldest one yelled, accomplishing not only a hearty laugh-about but the attention of the bartender, who yelled back, "Ready for another round?"

"We've been ready!" the young lady hollered, holding up an empty mug.

"Bring our friend here a beer, too!" added the old one, Jamen, nodding toward Ron. "Grab a seat here, young fellow!"

Thus began a full three hours (with a full four beers) of education for Ron, as well as some lighthearted fun with some disheartening topics. The five agents included a corridor manager (Jamen), two biologists, a wildlife technician, and one ranger (the young lady, Cove). There was plenty of small talk and joking at first—perhaps a beer's worth—but then the conversation turned serious, and the topics flowed naturally from a crew of such particular expertise. It started with some basic factoids.

The Mesoland Agency did snake surveys along the northern fenceline four times a year, and the counts had increased each year since 2128. It was early July now—July 2, 2145, to be precise—and back in April a team of agency biologists had counted 83 adult Burmese pythons and 14 northern boas along a five-mile stretch east of Memphis and not far from the train station. Furthermore, and crucially, "containment" wasn't always successful. In fact, the Mesoland Agency's mission statement included "the containment of dangerous wildlife within the Corridor and, when necessary, the destruction of dangerous wildlife north of the Corridor."

Along much of the corridor, "dangerous wildlife" meant pythons, primarily, and boas to a lesser extent. There were notable exceptions, though. About 80 miles east of Memphis was an area bluntly nicknamed No

Man's Land where the Agency tried to contain not only pythons and boas but anacondas, alligators, and crocodiles (American and even Nile, thanks to an utterly irresponsible zookeeper in Chattanooga) that came up the Tennessee River. Even piranhas were a problem in some stretches of the river; the Agency had largely given up on controlling them.

Factoids merged into concepts, and little by little Ron learned about global heating, "ecological integrity," biodiversity loss, and invasive species. He was introduced to terms such as "competitive exclusion," "niche breadth," "trophic levels," and "molecular clock." He also heard a lot about the lay of the land and the broader ecosystems of the South, tumultuous as they were in the 22nd century. He received, in essence, a four-beer degree in ecology and evolutionary studies, with a minor in biogeography.

Ron realized he'd never be able to remember half of what Jamen and the crew had told him, but he'd mull things over while they were fresh, and hang onto a few factoids that could come in handy. He was fascinated by one of the biologists in particular, an intense Afro-Latino woman who described the "evolutionary chaos" taking place in the tropical regions of Earth, including Mesoland and the containment corridor, which was now considered tropical in an ecological sense, if not geographically. Sounding more like a professor than a bureaucrat, the biologist (Makayla) professed, "Such chaos can only be understood in the broader context of life on Earth. Think of those polar bears forced off the North Pole and out into oblivion," resonating with Ron, who'd heard about the polar bear extinction as the Arctic ice had broken up. "What took their place? And what took the place of the grizzlies in Montana, as they in turn moved into the Arctic? And the black bears behind them? It's like a conveyor belt to extinction." Ron hadn't really thought of it like a conveyor belt, but now he'd never forget it. "Now just play a little leapfrog backwards, down to the Equator, and what do you have left to fill in for the mammals down there, most of which were already imperiled before global heating?"

Ron rubbed his chin and squinted his eyes, and Jamen yelled, "See that damn conveyor belt Ron?!"

"I don't want to oversimplify this," the mostly sober (and totally sobering) Makayla continued, "but about all you have left at the Equator is reptiles on land and fish in the sea, plus a few heat-tolerant bird species that can escape when they need to. The mammals are all out now; all the amphibians too except maybe a few tiger frogs, and that's a long story.

"Of course, that leaves the invertebrates: insects and arthropods and microorganisms like protozoa and bacteria. Plus, plants, algae... maybe some fungi. And the invertebrates have these really fast molecular clocks—lots of mutations happening all the time—and short breeding cycles, so they're evolving at the speed of light, if that's not an oxymoron..."

"Hold it a second!" Ron interrupted a little loudly, now into his fourth and final beer, "I'm losing you there. So, the mammals are gone, birds mostly gone, and now it's snakes and fish and bugs?!"

"You're catchin' on fast!" Jamen whooped.

"But then that molecular clock thing...what's that all about?"

"Basically," Makayla summarized, "With such frequent mutation and fast reproduction, the insects are evolving and adapting the fastest to global heating, so they're starting to dominate, on land at least. That makes for a plentiful food source for the smaller species of snakes, which the bigger species prey upon. So you've got three trophic levels from invertebrates to little snakes to big snakes."

"Snakes alive!" Cove shouted, almost pulling out her pistol for effect, but wisely deciding at the last instant to pantomime a shot to the floor instead. The group had a long hearty laugh, with the technician lurching away from the table and "shooting" at the ground as well.

"I think you got 'im!" Jamen yelled, and the group broke up, Tectonicas all showing 10:22.

Ron needed to find a hotel, and the Mesoland crew was headed to a bunkhouse on federal land south of town. Unlike Ron, the crew would be taking the

Special all the way to the Containment Corridor the next day. For the next three months, they would comprise the human presence at corridor's edge, mostly holed up at the research facility but venturing out for the quarterly snake survey and sending out drones for trap-checking in the corridor. Ron wished them all a safe tour of duty and thanked them vigorously for their hospitality and advice. They were one of the most unique little groups he'd ever encountered; they definitely occupied their own niche (as he'd come to know the term).

"Remember," Jamen warned, smiling yet clearly more serious now, "If you do see a python, run like hell unless it's fat. If it's fat, get some help and kill that sonofabitch."

How could Ron forget? Greeted by heat, he exited the dimly lit 1907 Tavern to an even dimmer street and a downright dark horizon. He found himself instinctively checking the ground around him; essentially and effectively the same ground upon which the crew had been "shooting snakes" a minute earlier. In the tavern the snake-shooting scene was funny, if not hilarious; out here the four beers and the fun had vanished like the sun. Instead of walking west in search of lodging, Ron hailed the nearest mule-cart driver and said, "Take me to a good hotel, please."

"Right to the front door," the driver uncannily added.

Luke Perrins

The next morning, over a coppee-chicory concoction in the dining room of the Highlander Hotel, Ron made his decision. He just had to get out on the ground, in the woods, on his own two feet in the heat of a South he would bring back to Tang in stories and in song...well maybe not so much in song, as he hated singing. But definitely in stories and perhaps in spirit as well. Back in the air-conditioned daylight, armed with ecological information, and on the heels of a hearty night at the 1907, he felt alive and emboldened; more so than at any time since he'd left New York, and maybe since leaving Alaska. He still had five more days allotted to his time in Tennessee, prior to a north-bound return from Nashville. So, for the next few days at least, he'd eschew the train, explore as much as he could by foot (or other means as handy) and find his way back to Nashville however he might. Instead of continuing to New York, though, he'd head straight to Chicago on the *Midwest Express* with only two stops en route: one in Louisville and one in Cincinnati.

Yes, he'd head straight to Chicago. Chicago and Julia.

All of it might be easier said than done, though. He'd only get so far on foot, especially in this ruthless heat, and it turned out there weren't many horse or mule-cart drivers willing to venture far into Tennessee. He eventually found a two-horse team with a driver who immediately cast doubt, "Don't know why you'd want to go down there, mister. Nothin' down there but big snakes, nasty women, and...well what's the difference?" Ironically enough, he took the job, explaining, "If you're crazy enough fer the payin', reckon I'm crazy enough fer the drivin'."

Soon the pair were clip-clopping south along hilly, well-worn roads, with kudzu encroaching en masse. Tennessee wasn't far at all for a two-horse cart, though, and just before noon they spotted a sign—half promotional, half navigational—that said, "T for Tectonica, T for Tennessee." The driver grumped, "Plenty of T, but damn little C for Coldon," which prompted in Ron an unpleasant thought of the Caldor family, if not of Tang at large.

A few hours later they reached the town of

Ridgetop and the driver announced, "End of the road for me, mister. You might find another driver at the Shaggy Saloon over there, but if you was to start walkin' like you was talkin' about, this here stretch down east of Nashville'd be your best bet. Snakes aren't so bad this high up, and yer gonna get water at a couple of springs. The road gets patrolled by the Tennessee Game Police, too. If you get in a pinch just use your EmergenT button. Wished I still had my Tectonica; dropped 'er in a sump last year."

Ron paid the driver, dropped by the Shaggy Saloon, and steeled himself for a very long walk. He'd learned from the cast of characters in recent days that Tennessee hikers had a trade-off to consider. They could hike at night to escape the worst of the heat, but pythons were most active at night, too. Obviously, there were other factors as well—bandits, visibility, available of services—but the big trade-off was between heat and snakes. Not that nighttime was cool and daytime snakeless, but as for the odds, the difference between night and day was the difference between snakes and heat.

To Ron, the decision at hand was a real dandy with a long list of complicating factors. As opposed to early morning (for a daylight hike) or sunset (nighttime hike), it was mid-afternoon. So, he could start off for Nashville now, and more or less split the risk between the heat (first few hours) and snakes (he'd be hiking most of the night). He could instead wait for morning, but there was only one, shaggy-looking hotel, next to the Shaggy Saloon. He might get a poor night's sleep there, making for a grueling hike in the sun tomorrow. Right now, he was still fairly refreshed—not tired at least—but then he'd be tired in the middle of the night; not the best condition for being alert for snakes. And what about bandits? Somewhat surprisingly, he'd heard little about that on this stretch; evidently the Tennessee Game Police were prevalent indeed.

Ron finally philosophized, if all these factors seemed to cancel each other out, it probably mattered little if he started out now or in the morning. For Ron, that meant the time was now! He bought $350 (three bottles) of water at the saloon, had a short chat with the bartender for any last, local advisories, checked the connection of his Tectonica, and commenced to marching south.

There was one word to best describe the first four hours of the walk: Hot! Walking almost due south, the sun was quartered off to his right, seemingly forever frying the front of his face and then, most especially, the side of it. By no means was he reckless enough to go bare-headed, but plenty of solar radiation reflected off the dirt road, which had a substantial share of light-colored lime. The temperature hovered around 120 degrees and Ron found himself sweating like Officer Gutierrez in the Wyoming sun and Levi from the

Southern Special combined. For a while, in the nebulous transition from late afternoon to early evening, he literally thought he might not make it, at least not without punching the EmergenT button (presuming it would work and the game police reached him in time).

Plodding slowly, head down (as it would have been anyway, for snake-sighting purposes), he saw a glimmer of water! "It must be one of the springs the driver mentioned," Ron thought with relief. He still had a bottle of water left, but that was far from sure to get him to the next watering hole. Why not fill the two empty bottles while he had the chance?

The water was pooled about fifteen feet from the west edge of the road; the pool itself was about fifteen feet across. Ron stopped, hands on knees, and peered into and all around it. The area around the pool was scraped out, and kudzu-shaped shadows covered half of it. The water looked neither clean nor dirty; water could be hard to assess with kudzu shade, glare from the sun, and a limestone base. He was as certain as he'd ever be, however, that there were no snakes in the cleared area, and said to the air, "So far so good." He stepped down off the roadway, onto the dusty dirt of the miniature basin, and with a few more steps, paused at the very edge of the water, leaning over it slightly for a closer look.

He wasn't quite sure just what he'd do yet when he heard a voice to his right, "I wouldn't do that if I were you."

Ron whipped his head around to see a skinny, bearded fellow standing at the edge of the scrape. He wore tattered bib overalls over a shallow chest and a tattered-to-match blue bandana around frizzy grey hair. "That hole is still polluted from the old strip mine," he said. "You put a foot in there and it's not gonna come out the same."

"Thanks for the warning," Ron replied, hastily retreating from the water. "I didn't see you. Are you from around here?"

"I'm from south of Nashville. I like to come up here for the cooler air sometimes." Ron was astounded by the "cooler air" phrase. "The name's Luke Perrins, by the way, and I was just making supper. Care to join me?"

Luke seemed genuine, nice, and hospitable. Ron had a good feeling about him, so he replied, "Lead the way, Luke. I'm Ron Neuwirth." Soon they were sitting on a fallen tree near a campfire, over which a small animal was roasting on a spit. Ron had never seen one before (neither the animal nor a spit, in fact).

"It's a nice, plump possum, so there'll be plenty for the both of us. My great grampa used to hunt deer around here, and my grampa still got a turkey or two. For my pa and me, though, it's mostly down to possum, at least aside from rat and snake. Pretty soon it might be all snake because the snakes are eatin' all the rats and possums!"

Ron thought there must be a few other species, but he couldn't imagine what they'd be, so he kept his mouth shut.

"Anyways, I was pretty lucky to get this one in the snare this morning. I still got some snake jerky in the pack over there if you wanna try that, too."

Ron opined he'd prefer the possum and was glad he did. The possum was better than he could have expected, especially served up with some greens that Luke had managed to pick. He seemed like a knowledgeable, resourceful survivalist.

"Is it true what they say about Nashville, that it's really gone downhill?" Ron asked as the fire burned low.

"Hell yes. Things got so hot, you couldn't even walk on the sidewalk in the daytime," Luke answered. "People who couldn't afford air conditioning just collapsed or wandered around, all dizzy and disoriented. It looks kind of funny but, believe me, you don't want to get heat stroke. I had it once and it will mess you up! I'm one of the lucky ones; lots of folks die from it in these parts.

"The Cumberland River is just about dry. Water's rationed, but people are always dipping into the river for bathing and washing dishes.

"Anyway, most people are long gone. The music industry moved all the way to northern Michigan. Did you ever hear of the Grand Ol' Opry?" (Ron hadn't.) "For a long time, they kept it up as a museum, more or less, but they finally ghosted it out in 2113. 'The day the music died' they called it, even though the Opry hadn't had a live showing for decades.

"Once the Opry was ghosted, it took about two months before half the town was looted. Most buildings were abandoned by then anyway. Come to think of it, there weren't a lot of looters, because there weren't many people left at all! Guess that's why only half the town was looted.

"But, some folks stayed, including ma and pa, and I'm still here too. Even a near-ghost-town is better than a wiped-out place, like 90 percent of old Florida and most of Louisiana."

"That's really depressing, Luke. I wish I could have seen it all before the Wasteful, or even before the Industrial Revolution. I wonder what it looked like!

Luke simply said, "Yeah, they really screwed us with the Wasteful. You know what though, Ron? I'm going to visit some friends over by Murfreesboro tomorrow. That's a bit of a trip, but we don't have to walk the whole way. My sister Sara has a couple of old mules she'd lend us. She lives just down the road here apiece. We can make it there by midnight, and we're lucky there's a half moon a-waxing. Two people is better with snakes, too; the vibration confuses 'em a bit. I've never heard of a python grabbin' anyone unless they were alone. Of course, you could still always get stung by a rattler, and that's no picnic either, but nothin's worse than a crusher."

"Crusher," Ron hadn't heard that one yet, either. "Great." True to Luke's word, though, they made it to Sara's place with no crusher incidents. No rattlers either. Sara unfolded a cot for Ron, who thanked her and fell asleep ten minutes later.

The next morning, Ron struggled to balance himself on the back of a big grey animal that didn't seem anxious to go anywhere. He'd never ridden horseback, much less with a mule. Luke traveled in front of him on an even bigger, browner beast. "You don't have to worry about Sam taking off on you. That's the good thing about mules; they don't do anything more than they have to or want to. And they hardly ever want to move fast."

Luke made some clicking sounds, mule code evidently, and his mule Jake finally got going. Sure enough, Sam followed. They traveled on dirt roads most of the time. "I try to stay off the old highways," Luke explained, "because it's too hard on their feet. A lot of the old concrete is broken and heaved, which makes it kind of risky too. Plus, the snakes like that pavement, especially earlier in the day before it gets too hot even for a snake!" The two men and beasts had to take their time, stopping to rest in the shade every so often. Neither of them carried a thermometer, but Luke said, "She'll be all of 120 today." Ron knew he wasn't talking about the price of water (although it would be close for that as well).

As they plodded along, Ron saw old homes, big and small, almost all of which were abandoned. "If you don't mind squatting, you can find yourself a mighty fine house to settle in. That is, if you don't mind going without electricity and running water," Luke said.

Ron also noticed that there didn't seem to be any stores per se, nowhere en route to Murfreesboro at least. Occasionally he saw the ruins of old country stores, and one even had a rusty old gasoline pump. Luke gave it the finger and blurted, "Way to go you Wasteful bastards!" Cars were still found here and there—the Tennessee Game Police used little pickup trucks even—but Luke had never driven a car in his life, and never would.

They eventually came to a big bridge with a plastic sign in the middle that read: Percy Priest Lake. "Is that really a lake down there?" Ron inquired. "It looks more like a mud puddle."

"Sure is—or was," Luke responded. "They say back in the Wasteful it was 42 miles long with 15,000 acres of water; 100 feet deep in spots, too. All year long, every year. Well, it doesn't take too many years at 120 to scoop all that water right up into the clouds. Now when it rains, it *rains*, and I've seen this place flooded to the bridge, believe it or not. But no, it's the heat that gets the better of that deal. And I've seen 'er up to 130, now."

They finally reached the outskirts of Murfrees-boro, and Luke pulled his mule to a stop in front of a small store. "Wow, a store," Ron observed, oblivious to the obviousness. Barrels of fruits he'd never seen—lychee, jackfruit, dragon fruit— and one plastic carton of peaches were displayed on the porch. Inside were weathered hand tools adorning the walls. Most were covered in rust, but they all had prices. The shelves had greens and vegetables, hands of tobacco, and cans of beans and tomatoes. One shelf near the counter was labeled "Jerky," but it was empty. "People like their snake jerky around here," Ron pointed out.

"Boa's the best, but really they're all pretty good if you ask me."

"I'll take your word for it, now," Ron replied, testing out the tiniest of Tennessee expressions he thought he'd detected.

Luke chuckled at that and headed to the counter, where he gave a hearty elbow bump to the owner, the only other person in the store. "Great to see you, Frank. This boy here is a visitor from the north, come to see how the other half lives. I figured you could give him an earful."

Frank replied, "Well, maybe I can, and I probably will, if you haul him on down to the hoedown later."

"That I will, now, that I will," promised Luke.

Hoedown

The hoedown that night was on the road to Hoodoo, almost there in fact. If Hoodoo ever had a suburb, this was it: a line of shanties and a makeshift graveyard. Plus, low and behold, on an old parallel, paved road just west of the shanties, in a grove of massive eucalyptus trees, stood an ancient, antebellum plantation house. As Luke and Ron pulled up on their mules, a lively crowd of people poured out. "We were afraid you weren't comin'," Jubal said. "A Perrins hoedown just ain't the same without some real music!" Then, with a glance toward Ron, "Who's this feller?"

"Ron here is a visitor from the north side, way up in the Upper U.S. of A., and I mean way up. He wanted to see what things were like down here. You gotta give him credit for the effort. Maybe when he gets back to his fancy digs and rich neighbors, they'll help us out a little," Luke winked at Ron.

"They better!" Jubal yelled, sounding one beer up on the rest, herding the crowd back into the house. People plopped themselves down in the assortment of battered chairs and couches in a huge great room. Some headed for a buffet of sorts, laid out on an antique but indestructible billiards table. The assortment started out with greens, moved into some hot-country vegetables and meats, and ended at a 20-gallon plastic drum of high-octane raisin jack. Off to one side were some fruits in a plastic basket and a barrel of home-brewed beer, strong with the smell of spelt. Ron could identify none of it aside from the beer.

Luke interrupted the proceedings by banging a big tin spoon against a huge bowl of collards and shouting, "This here's Ron Neuwirth from way up north! He's a friend of mine and a friend of ours. He's never been to a hoedown, so let's be on our best behavior!" The latter admonition elicited a wide range of comments, but all were in good cheer.

Ron felt a little apprehensive, being the only one (evidently) from the North. In a way, he was glad he was from "way" up north, as Luke kept putting it, because it might seem more like another universe than a rival region to the Perrins clan. Maybe that was even Luke's intention, and Ron was grateful. Either way he'd have some explaining to do, if he got roped into it, about the filthy riches and extreme advantages on Tang. His anxiety subsided somewhat when it became apparent the guests were in a jovial mood, lubricated by the jack or the beer (or both, in some cases).

Ron snagged an old wooden chair with a thread-bare velvet seat, and before he could contemplate a trip to the mystery buffet, an unusually well-dressed man plunked a folding chair down next to him. "Howdy Ron," he said. "I'm Zander Ludlow."

"Hi," Ron said as they elbow-bumped. "You're not a Perrins then?"

"No, and I'm actually from Massachusetts," helping Ron to feel like he wasn't the only one from a lot further north.

"Massachusetts! How did you end up here?" Ron was intrigued. Massachusetts, while technically not in the Upper USA, was "next tier down" along with states like Oregon, Iowa, and New Jersey. In ancient, ante-bellum terms, these states (especially the latter) were about as far from the "South" as New York or Connecticut. The decision of the 144th Congress in 2076 to parse Upper from Lower America that far north, leaving three "New England" states in Lowmerica, was one of the most contentious and painful processes ever undertaken by the American polity. It could have triggered a civil war, except the political stakes were so mixed up along the "Tier Line" from West to East, alliances were almost impossible to conceive of, much less implement and arm.

"It had to be done" became a political rallying cry of "Top Tier" politicians, who saw a hopeless wave of ecological upheaval in the Deep South triggering an equally hopeless wave of social upheaval almost everywhere further north. If the USA was to remain a cogent polity, and without invading Canada, it had to retrench in the Top Tier and hold the line. Two lines really: the Mesoland Containment Corridor and the Tier Line.

One problem the ecological upheaval of Mesoland had "solved," in the most existentially devastating way, was the "Latino onrushes" of the early Wasteful. Central America was gone, as were the lower-lying regions of northern South America. At this point in history, the only substantial Latino emigrations were south of the tropics into Bolivia, Chile, Argentina, and Uruguay. Meanwhile, north of Mesoland, with the Containment Corridor running southwesterly, only a wedge of Mexico comprising the old states of Chihuahua, Sonora, and Baja California remained. These were some of the hottest climes on Earth, and Mexican holdouts were reduced to the highest valleys in the Mexican Rockies, plus a few shoreline pockets of Sonora and the Baja.

Of course, none of these matters of bio-political geography were running through the beleaguered mind of Ron, who was hoping his new acquaintance could help him with some cultural bearings.

Zander answered with, "Well, I got a journalism degree in Boston College when it was still open, and then worked for a few T-papers in New England." (Tectonica had taken over the remaining print-mode news coverage, using plastipaper manufactured by Swinton Plastics.) "I came down here for a story on the Containment Corridor, but I gravitated toward Tennessee culture, in my writing and personally too. I hate it down here, but I love it, too. It's hotter than hell, everything's in short supply, and the damn snakes will drive you nuts if they don't kill you first. But here's the thing, Ron: *It's not crowded!*"

That explained a lot, Ron thought, and resonated more. Ever since departing Tang on the *Chakirya*, Ron had spent half the trip exhausted by heat and humidity, half the trip exhausted by the crowds, and most of the trip overwhelmed by the combination of both.

In a three-minute trip down memory lane, and narrating for Ron, Zander described how he'd covered much of the major news as an earlier journalist: political fireworks across the Tier Line, the Boston T Party (when a loose-knit Massachusetts militia threw their Tectonicas into the sea), the christening of the containment corridor, and the death of a Memphis mayor at the coils of a python.

"Plus," Zander concluded, "I wrote a deep dive into the plight of the people down here. It bugs me to this day. I T-mailed it all off to the Associated Monitors, and they turned it down! They were the last deep-dive syndicate left, and they had some editors who were really interested. I'm guessing the censors—same ones who controlled the ten-second outlets like T-News and P-Scene—had gotten to the AM as well, and they didn't want anything in the news that was sympathetic to the South, or sympathetic to the poor anywhere, for that matter."

The misplaced Massachusetts journalist paused for a moment, looking down around his shoes, and concluded with, "Well, let's go get us some grub." The two new conversationalists headed for the collards and proceeded to the raisin jack (Zander) and the beer (Ron), then back to the folding and velvet chairs, respectively.

"Now what about you, Ron? Whatever brought you to Mesoland North?" Zander used one of the more depressing nicknames for Tennessee and the "bottom tier" states bordering the Corridor.

"Well, that's a long story, now," Ron started right in with his bit of Tennesseean. "To be honest, Zander, I'm from one of the richest places on the planet, called Tang, up in the Bering Sea." He wasn't ready to tell Zander or anyone among the Perrins clan that, not only had he come from this far-off rich place, but he was born into one of the 100 wealthiest families on Earth. Not yet at least. He'd bide his time, unless the beer bode it farewell. But for now, he stuck with, "I just had this urge to see what the rest of the world was like, or at least the 'Mericas. And, since Tang is way up north, I was even more interested in these parts here, the Deeeeep South." Ron continued to play up the other-world aspect of his origins, relative to the Tennesseans'. "I was actually hoping to spend a day or two in Mesoland, too, but when I started finding out how damn dangerous it is...count me out!"

Jubal's brother Clem, with no one else to talk to at the moment, happened to be in the conversational orbit. When Ron brought up the dangers of Mesoland, Clem blurted, "Kudzu, crushers, and Jesus Christ!" It was a common saying, close to the Corridor, the thought being that only the omnipotent Christ could survive in Mesoland. Only Jesus could plow through the swaths of kudzu, machete in hand, stepping on the heads of the pythons and loving everybody who wasn't there.

By now the rest of the room was peering in his direction when Ron reacted, "You mean 'Jesus Cristo?'" apparently in pure innocence, although no one could tell for sure, and everyone wondered at the Latinized pronunciation of the deity's name, by this fellow from way up north no less. The fact was, there was no religion whatsoever on Tang, except perhaps hidden among the workers. The 100 themselves were above and beyond any sort of religion, theology, or even religious history, so Ron had simply never heard of Jesus Christ. He had, however, the distinct memory of the sweating Officer Gutierrez in line for the Two-Room and had heard the expression among Latinos in Chicago as well (including once in a Two-Room). He developed his own vague idea of the Latino religion, centered around the Christo figure, but he never figured out why the name was used in frustration instead of celebration.

Right now, Ron felt the presence of a dozen stares in the midst of a palpable, pregnant pause, as the good folks of Hoodoo examined his expression for signs of ridicule, sarcasm, or heresy. When they saw nothing of the sort, but rather only a cross between confusion and embarrassment, the loudest communal guffaw of the entire evening broke out and ran for a solid minute. Thus was borne a new twist on an old expression in Hoodoo and beyond, "Kudzu, crushers, and Jesus Cristo!"

The talk went on with Ron, Zander, Clem, and a widening circle including the likes of Lucinda, Cove (not the Cove from the Mesoland Agency), Reppert, Frank from the store, Wenda, and the incredibly named Tennessee T Perrins, nicknamed Teety and jokingly portrayed as a shill for the Tectonica Corporation. By the end of everyone's eating, Luke and Jubal were in the mix as well. Elbow bumping, the life-saving habit developed during the COVID and peccary pox pandemics, had given way to vigorous handshakes and hugs. Not that it would have mattered at this point. The raisin jack and the beer had brought people toe-to-toe and nose-to-nose; the soberest among them hoped no one had the "vid" or the pox or any number of other infectious diseases. The crowd had more-or-less officially become raucous.

Ron was mulling over a question about the Two-Rooms on Tang when a young lady grabbed his arm. It was the "other Cove" (as Ron thought of it), who seemed to be even rowdier than the original, snake-shooting Cove. "Hey Ron, Luke's playin' the Hoedown Humdinger out there!" evidently referring to out in the heat, although at this point the Coldon was running low in the antebellum, anyway. "Can you dance Ron? If you can't, I'll teach you! I sure will, now!"

Ron was pulled into the back yard, halfway willingly he noticed, where couples were awhirl in a stomped-out, scraped out, torch-lit area the size of a Tangian swimming pool. As he fumbled his way through the Humdinger, the Cannonball Special, and a funny-sounding song called "Sailor's Hornpipe," he saw very little of his dance partner, by virtue of the speed of motion inherent to the selections, the auburn hair falling relentlessly over her face, and the advanced collection of beers in his belly. Oddly enough, given the proceedings thus far, a slow song came about, although Clem messed up the ambience with a disorienting blurt of "Kudzu, crushers, and Jesus Cristo!"

But now, under the glow of the torches and to the slow tune of "If We Make it to December," the other Cove came into focus before him, and she turned out to be nothing short of beautiful. She was about 20, slender and gently curved, and her wavy auburn hair fell just past her shoulders. She was tall for a lady; only two inches shorter than Ron, with her high cheekbones and her narrow nose brushing at times against his chin, his neck, and his ears. To top it off, the only things this green-eyed lady was wearing besides the shortest denim pants and the slightest tank top was a tasteful set of jewelry about her neck, ears, and one of her ankles. Ron had the quickest of questions for himself, "Is it the beer or the gear?" and instantly concluded it was neither (well maybe partly the beer), but rather everything else: the eyes, the nose, the hair, the curves. And, she had an attitude.

Once they'd made it through the lyrical December, and without further ado, Cove broke the celebratory mood with, "You want to know what things are like down here Ron? I can tell you some things that no one else can or will, now. My family moved over here from East Tennessee. You know, where the mountains are, those pretty mountains that everyone used to travel so far to see. The people there are really strugglin' to get by what with game bein' so scarce. You can't grow much in that rocky soil either, especially now that everything is either too dry or too wet. I do declare, Ron, it's either flooded or parched; ain't no in-between no more!

"Back in some of those valleys and hollows they don't have to worry about burying anyone, either, if you know what I mean. I've even heard of some of that happening right around here. Not many pets left in the mountains, either." This was beyond the pale for Ron; he'd only figure it out on the train back to Chicago.

"Yeah Ron, it's real dangerous. You heard about the decimators? These damn radicals...nobody can figure out where they came from, but I mean they are dead serious about what they call 'one-planet living.' Even after World War III and the one-child policy and the pandemics and all, they think the population is still too much! They wanna shrink it by half! They're heavily armed, too, with AR-45s and even gun-drones. When they take control of a town, they force a 'life lottery' and the losers are executed on the spot!"

Precisely at the moment when Ron wondered about the funeral arrangements of the "losers," Cove continued, "They do give the losers a choice of firing squad or poisoning, though. It's quick-lime so it's quick either way. But the winners gotta bury the dead, usually in a mass grave because nobody wants to give up any gardenin' space."

Cove paused and studied him for a moment, then shifted gears faster than a wind turbine in a Wyoming chinook.

"Hey Ron, you're not a bad-looking guy. Want a little company for your trip back up north, maybe? I don't eat much, now."

This too Ron would ponder on the train to Chicago. Were the conditions in the South so bad for women that they'd advertise themselves as slight consumers in order to get further north? Would they really go hungry just for the gamble of going less hungry in a crowded, noisy city that the Zanders of the world couldn't stand? Would they be sorry if they did make it to Chicago or New York or megalopolitan Milwaukee?

Suddenly, rashly, Ron's mind was awash with sympathy for Cove. She'd been so welcoming, so fun, so...attractive.

But Ron had Julia.

That said, Julia had a serious health condition that could spiral out of control as it had for half of the recipients of that first COVID-AK vaccine.

After a little of that back-and-forth, Ron's mind yelled, "Stop!" Cove was beautiful and Julia was sick, but Ron was drunk, and he needed...

Luke appeared just in time to hear Cove's advances. He tugged at Ron's shirt and said, "Hey, you gotta get some sleep, my friend. If you want that *Midwest Express* tomorrow, you better call it a night. We leave in the morning and it's gonna be a hot one."

That was exactly what Ron needed to hear, the first part at least. He needed some sleep, and he wanted some separation from the issue that had suddenly arose; namely, the tension between his love of Julia and the sudden attraction to Cove.

Luke showed Ron to a bunkhouse at the edge of the torchlight where about half the group would be sleeping on cots or plastic pads. "She's tight," Luke said of the house, patting the screen-door frame as they entered. The bunkhouse had been modified with screen doors on all four sides for nighttime "cooling" purposes. Ron had never slept on a plastic pad before, and the "T-Pad" (evidently a product of some kind of Swinton/Tectonica deal) was fine for an inebriated 20-year-old at the end of his first hoedown. A few hoe-downers were already snoring, as were Ron and Luke (the latter on a nearby cot) in a matter of minutes.

Cove was somewhere in the vicinity as well, including in the dreams of more than one hoedowner.

Python

Lying under the kudzu at the edge of a barren "water" hole, the python was virtually non-sentient. Not that she didn't have a glimmer of sentience in her life; she most certainly did have glimmers, but for the past ten days, she was out like a dead bulb 99 percent of the time, "satisfied" in the faintest yet thorough sense imaginable. The temperature was pleasant—nice and warm the whole time—and never cold. Not too hot either, certainly not for a crusher, as kudzu made for outstanding shelter. And all the while, the possum in her belly provided a slow buzz of energy.

The possum had been a big, lactating female. Now, the last vestiges of the possum were making their way through the python's digestive tract and into her circulatory system, from which they would gradually be pulled and transformed into additional muscle, nerve, and organ cells. Some items, like the BB cap embedded in the possum's butt, as well as much of the possum's bone tissue, would be passed out the python's anus when she began to move again. All in all, the possum had been a generous dose of calories and nutrients, keeping the python's #1 enemy at bay. That enemy was hunger.

Python sentience, not that it was extensive, was well-known among herpetologists (the scientists that studied reptiles and what few amphibians were left). The way they looked at it, for sentience purposes at least, a python was like a crawling man or woman, but with a limited set of sensations. For a python, there was no love and no hate. A python experienced no empathy, jealousy, humor, anger, or mischievousness. A python was totally "apolitical," you might say. On the other hand, a python literally felt pain, heat, cold, pressure, sound waves, and, as the closest thing to an emotion, fear.

Almost no one believed—although there was no way of being certain—that a python "thought" about any of these sensations at any level. A python wouldn't be thinking, "Holy hell it's hot out here. I better find some kudzu." Heat, pain, fear and the rest were so dimly perceived as to register only the slightest movement of a cognometer needle in the labs at Columbia University. In contrast, humans hooked up to cognometers consistently produced measurements above a thousand cognobytes. One way for a human to view it, then, was to think of the python as having similar senses to theirs (at least the non-emotional ones), but with an intensity of a thousandth or less if you could imagine such a thing.

While pythons moved through their world of encounters with the dimmest of sensations, such levels of sensation were all it "knew." As such, these sensations were everything to a python, and infinitely greater than those of a drone or even a robot. Furthermore, one sensation was felt strongly, relative to the other sensations at least. That sensation was its mortal enemy: hunger.

And so it was that, while Ron and Luke hiked to Sara's, slept overnight, and rode their mules to the hoedown, the python lay at the edge of the scrape, about 30 feet from a dusty, limey road. She was gradually waking up to her strongest sensation. As with humans, sensations overlapped and mixed, too. For a python, and outside of sex, the closest relative to hunger in its "family" of sensations was fear. Hunger drove a python with an urgency as if borne of fear.

A python's vision was as dim as its senses, but this python had started scouting the scrape visually in advance of its post-possum movements. Something was "wrong" about it, wrong with the place. Animals appeared—possums, hognose skunks, an armadillo once—but they backed away immediately and ran off faster than a firefly's flicker. The one exception was a tall critter that stood along the edge for a good half-minute. This one, with the particular infrared it emanated from head to toe, created a dim (even for a snake) stirring in the python, causing it to tongue the air for the first time that day. Yet even that critter ended up walking away, with none of the splashing around in the liquid that often forebode success for the python.

The python's circuitry was set now. As soon as the possum had done its part, she'd be moving on, like a heat-seeking warhead on a fully articulating, cold-blooded, ground-hugging, horizontal rocket. She'd think nothing of it, not at all about it. The hunger would simply launch her, and her movements would be described by the herpetologists as "lateral undulation" (aka "slithering"). Her collection of 52 midbody scales would be gripping grains of sand, pebbles, and rock surfaces in rapid-fire succession like the whirling treads of a tire on a speeding police truck.

As the sun touched its first kudzu leaf on the horizon, the python uncoiled itself and, with no sign left of a possum bump, she slithered across the scrape and up onto the road. Her navigational circuitry "told" her she'd never been further north, and that home base was south, so off she went on the road to Hoodoo, heading toward the half-moon in the southern sky.

The road was easy slithering, so she stuck to it almost exclusively. Her evening was mostly uneventful as she passed only a half dozen mice, two rats, a nighthawk, sundry lizards, four rattlesnakes and one other python, a smaller, disinterested male dispersing northward. Also, there were two tall critters, one moving north and one moving south, encountered about an hour apart. The one moving north passed her by with a wide berth; too wide a berth at too high a speed to develop an "interest" in. The one moving south did generate some interest, but as she approached him from the rear, the alert hiker, who looked in all directions constantly, gave a shout, emitting a harsh sound wave that temporarily stopped her in her tracks. Then, in the dimmest vision imaginable (to a human at least), she "watched" the hiker run like hell. Gone like a little lizard from a super-heated slab of slate, the hiker was never seen again. Not on the road at least.

Hours went by and hunger pushed the python relentlessly. Pythons weren't the fastest of snakes, but she was all of fourteen feet, so she could easily exceed the speed of a younger slitherer. Moving from two to three miles per hour, she'd reach Hoodoo before daybreak. Of course, she might not need to travel that far. She didn't "hope" to find food sooner, but hunger would push her to "try."

Just past midnight, she slithered up to a country

store, shut down for the night, but "open for business"
on the porch and along its foundation. Unmistakably
mammalian infrared signals had pulled her in, so she
checked it all out, "opting" for rectilinear locomotion,
a method that allowed for moving in nearly a straight
line and *as* nearly a straight line. She was like a stick
on the ground, a forward-moving stick with a forked
tongue. She'd "found," thanks to the evolution of her
forebears, the perfect way to move along straight edges like walls and fences, porches, and foundations. It
not only worked in tight quarters, but it was silent.
Deadly silent. Boas were still the best at it, and needed
to be, as they were pure stalkers. But most predatory
snakes (and which snakes weren't?) could pull this trick
out of their behavioral bag, and pythons were accom-
plished rectiliners.

Pythons were often thought of as "ambush hunt-
ers" in the ancient ecological texts of the pre-Wasteful,
but they were much more than that, especially by 2145.
They'd been evolving and adapting too, especially in
Mesoland. No, not as quickly as the insects with their
speedy "molecular clocks," as the biologist Makayla was wont to describe in the taverns of Tennessee,
but quickly enough to diversify their behavior and
expand their niche. They'd always been quite capable
of stalking, like their distant brethren boas, and at this
point in their evolutionary history, they were just as
likely to stalk as to ambush. They weren't yet capable

of "racing" to catch moving prey, like their cousins the racers, but they could do the line crawl and catch unsuspecting animals with the best of 'em.

That said, on this particular evening at this particular store, all her best rectilining was largely for naught. Other than a mouse (which she did lap up, as a man might grab a peanut from a bowl between lunch and dinner), a couple of escaping lizards, and a gazillion insects, she detected nothing of caloric interest. She had no "curiosity" in anything else—antique or plastic or made in China—so no time was wasted between here and Hoodoo.

One incident that did cost her time—and calories—happened about halfway between the store and Hoodoo. A Tennessee Game Police officer was patrolling the stretch with fog lights only, to avoid far-off detection by poachers and other ne'er-do-wells. By this point in the history of the TGP, "patrolling" amounted largely to counting snakes, reporting snakes, and killing snakes. "Count 'em and kill 'em" was the unofficial motto. Vaguely reminiscent of "Who's on First," TGP officers (as well as Cove from the Mesoland Agency gang) would argue philosophically about the proper order and classification. Did you count one that was killed? If you counted one, then killed it, should you count it again or just re-categorize it? What if you stumbled upon a killed one? How would you know if it had been counted already? "Counted or Killed?" was a distant second (so to speak) from Who's on First, for sheer humor, but the game police stuck to a wildlife theme, so "Counted or Killed?" it was.

The python felt the road vibration long before it sensed the fog lights. She hadn't achieved her 14 feet without an encounter or two with the TGP (and vehicles in general), so she'd positioned herself along the side of the road by the time the fog lights reached her. The TGP officers were seasoned, quick, and alert, though. The truck stopped on a dime and, before you could get to "Two Mississippi," they'd each jumped out with implements in hand. The officer on the passenger's side was shining a spotlight at the python, while the driver was pumping a shell into a semi-automatic 12-gauge shotgun. Before you could get to "Three Mississippi," the python was off the side of the road and slithering like hell for the cover of the kudzu. At precisely "Four Mississippi" the first report of the 3-inch magnum could be heard most of the way to Hoodoo, while the contents of the shell (212 #5 pellets) tore a hole in a fire-ant nest just west of the python. The second shot, though, came much closer to "Good night Eilish," and two pellets stung her in the tail.

The "tail" of a snake was also philosophical material for the TGP. Was it everything below the head? If so, nearly all shots were tail shots, but that seemed overly demanding if the goal was a head shot. Was the tail precisely the back half, thus dividing the snake evenly between head and tail? Alternatively, was it only the little bit behind the cloaca ("anus" in lay terms)? When you thought about it much, it gained in import, too, because "head" became similarly unclear, and if the officer wanted to claim a head shot, the dividing line (jaw, heart, liver) mattered. The biggest cheaters called it a head shot if it was anywhere but the tail, furthermore opting for the halfway point as the dividing line between heads and tails.

The officer this evening tended to be honest, though, and yelled, "Shit, tail shot!"

The other officer repeated the "Shit" part, followed by, "Let's get the hell out of here!" Neither one of them was crazy enough to crawl into the kudzu with a tail-shot crusher, especially one such as this. "Did you see that sonofabitch?" he continued inside the cab. It wasn't a well-thought question: Given the first officer had actually shot the sonofabitch, he must have at least seen it. What the officer really meant was, "Did you see the *size* of that sonofabitch?" In any event, he continued, "He must have been a 20-footer," getting the sex and the size of the crusher quite wrong in the course of six words.

"Well," the senior officer said from behind the wheel, "I don't know if he was *that* long. But damn near. Hopefully I re-jiggered his circuitry a bit. I wouldn't mind pythons so much if they'd just stay away from trucks and houses and people. They eat a lot of rats, and they make some fine jerky, now."

"That they do, now; that they do."

While the TGP truck continued north, the python continued on south, a stinging in her tail that was mostly eclipsed by the hunger enveloping her. On her quest for calories, the incident with the TGP would turn out fateful. She'd quartered off to the southwest and slithered onto a parallel road which, here and there, contained patches of the concrete it once comprised fully. The concrete patches felt good along her belly, plenty warm as they were, and made for efficient slithering. Cracks in the pavement held plenty of giant jumping worms; "Alabama jumpers" some still called them, despite the fact that Alabama was a memory more than a place, fully below the corridor and forever consigned to Mesoland. The jumpers weren't sufficient for the python to stop and gorge on them, especially with the mechanical difficulty of scooping them up and out of the cracks, but where extra-wide cracks and Alabama jumpers coincided, the python stopped ever so briefly for appetizers.

Approximately an hour after the moon set, off toward the anachronistically named Beechgrove (beeches having been consigned to northern Canada by now), the python pulled up to a wood-and-plastic structure with "interesting" infrared all about. She quickly shifted gears into rectilinear motions, moving silently along the cut shale comprising the foundation. Suddenly, however, a blast of infrared wafted directly over her head, and the closest thing to exhilaration a snake could feel (which wasn't very close at all, in human cognometric terms) came upon her. It didn't assuage her hunger one bit, but rather synergized it in a way that put her in proper predatory mode. You might say it transformed her driving hunger into "positive energy."

The humans who'd created this structure knew a lot about snakes. The place was "tight," as they put it in snake country, with no holes bigger than the diameter of an AR-45 shell. Windows were high up and inoperable due to multiple careless paint jobs. The doorframes, though, were fit with a mastery that would have impressed Frank Lloyd Wright. Each of the four frames was occupied by perfectly fitting screen doors; thus, the wafting, which happened to be coming out the easternmost door, right over and around the python's approving head. The python further tested the airways with her tongue, depositing the molecules inside her mouth for purposes of "tasting" prospective foodstuffs. In the simplest terms of a barely sentient snake, these molecules were "good."

Skilled, smart carpenters (two of the three at least) had built the bunkhouse two feet off the ground using cut slate stones on the ground, with smooth, A-Grade plastic blocks atop the stones. No snake would find any purchase along these blocks, and small snakes didn't stand a chance of reaching a doorsill, which in any event would be blocked by a tightly fitting door. But the python was no small snake and needed no purchase on the plastic. It had yet another means of locomotion in its behavioral collection: the concertina.

The concertina really came in handy for climbing smooth eucalyptus trees or even smooth steel poles. It wouldn't work for climbing straight up a high smooth wall, but for the 14-foot python, only the first stretch forward—the neck stretch— was needed to position her head at the doorsill. And position it thusly she did.

The carpenters were smart, but they'd been drinking spelt beer the day they built the bunkhouse, and they'd saved the eastern door for last, so they could work in the shade around sunset. By then they were inebriated, hungry, hasty, and overconfident. The sequence of small errors they'd commit while framing the fourth doorway would go overlooked, partly because the youngest carpenter was expected to do the bulk of the framing for this final door, having learned from the two older ones throughout the day. Not the brightest of the three bulbs, he glanced numerous times at the frame directly across the bunkhouse for a reference and proceeded admirably in reproducing that frame to a T, a Tennessee T as it were. It all looked smooth enough to the other two, who by now were more concerned with draining the last of the spelt beer before the big Coldon cooler was spent. Some horseplay erupted at this point, which further distracted the Tennessee three. Summarily the door was hung—hinges, handle and all—and the Tennessee three headed back out the western door to collect their tools and ride on back to Hoodoo.

Thenceforth, not a single hoedowner did a thing about the fact that the eastern door swung inward, not outward! Nine out of ten never even noticed it; anyone else forgot about it after a glass of raisin jack.

And now, as the python came eyeball to eyeball with a mosquito she couldn't even see on the bottom panel of the door, she instinctively placed the front of her head, right between the two nostrils, against the door panel. Silently and smoothly like only a snake could. The well-crafted (albeit backwards) door moved, just as silently and smoothly as the python. Now, after a combination of slithering with her tail, concertina motions with her mid-section, and rectilining with her "head and neck" over and beyond the threshold, the bunkhouse hosted 9 warm bodies of 110 pounds or more (not all warm-blooded but all very warm), including a 130-pound python.

The crusher was just getting started. That forceful hunger and that dim exhilaration brought her westward still, toward a wave of irresistible infrared, until her bottom jaw touched the top corner of a T-pad. The infrared was almost overwhelming now. Furthermore, the best of it was only a foot away!

A python (perhaps unlike some rookie TGP officers) never mistook heads and tails, or heads and feet
as it were, even in pitch dark. Herpetologists would
never get to the bottom of this uncanny ability, but it
had something to do with the gradient of infrared between the head area (with waves flowing liberally from
ears, cheeks, and neck) and the rest of the body, which
was far more stubborn in releasing its heat. By the time
a python was ready to strike, it knew exactly where to
strike. It never thought to itself, "I see. Now there's that
spot, right between those two heat-emitting ears, that I
will henceforth pounce upon." It simply struck the bullseye, only rarely missing.

All snakes have the ability to strike. That's basically their thing. A garter snake will strike a mouse.
A rat snake will strike a chicken. A small python will
strike a rat. But, a huge python, especially when ini-
tiating contact with a large prey animal that it can't
simply chomp off the ground, would be much better
described as "hammering" or "pounding" its prey. The
ideal hammering motion (for the python's sake, that is)
is precisely over the top of the head. Under some conditions, the blow can break the neck of the unsuspecting animal, immobilizing it quickly, making for a safer
job the rest of the way out.

Not that the python hammers and hammers
and pounds and pounds, like a carpenter framing up
a house. It takes just one hammering motion, and the

python has the head of the prey tightly in its jaws. It's not a crushing machine just yet—not like a crocodile or alligator that can crush with its jaws—but it will be within two seconds as the rest of the snake coils around the neck and torso, like a three-D slingshot slinging in all directions, constricting so rapidly and so forcefully that no more breaths will be taken after "Three Mississippi."

And so, as the Hoodoo-hoedown python touched the corner of Ron's T-pad, she surely would have thought (if only pythons thought like humans), "Oh, this is gonna be good!"

At that very moment, Ron's dreamworld was coming undone. His lovely Julia was over to the left, arms extended for a hug, while the coveted Cove was off to the right, blowing him a kiss. It had been coming to this for an eternity of dreamtime, and he just couldn't take it anymore. He split right in half, like a round of tulip poplar under a splitting maul (which by now would occur only in northern Canada). His right arm shot crazily to the right; his left one flapped frantically to the left. Evidently, he wanted it all—an impossibility for sure—and it made him berserk, which was further evidenced by his yelling of "Julecove, Covelia, Covejule" and such.

Ron's fit woke up the other seven humans (albeit some only for seconds), and it scared the snakeshit out of the python. Not literally, of course, and the "fear" would have registered so faintly on a cognometer as to barely bear witness, but in the python's world it was everything in that moment. The moment was so profoundly frightful, in snake-fright terms, it even eclipsed her hunger as a motivational force. No time for rectilining now, or even "thinking" about it; she slithered at top speed straight ahead until, as luck would have it, she was headed over the western doorsill and back out onto the Tennessee turf she'd so temporarily transcended.

No one would ever know about the incident, for no one fully awake had spotted the snake, and she left no sign whatsoever of her entry or exit. Certainly, no sign detectable by any of the hungover hoedowners.

As for the python, hunger quickly resumed its control over her night, which by now was approaching first light. A handful of the more reckless, careless, desperate, or drunken hoedowners had flopped on the ground for the night. Some of them had a sense of security in numbers that was roughly as undeveloped (thanks to the raisin jack) as a snake's sense of smell. The python passed close enough to several of these bodies to sense some infrared. Cove was among them; Jubal too. Finally, just as the proportion of hunger to fear reached critical mass, with the slithering back down to a moderate pace, the python detected another body that just might be "the one."

Cove had been on the left, and Jubal on the

right; this one was straight ahead. The infrared pattern was quite like theirs, too, with more waves than Cove had emitted, and slightly less than Jubal's. The python stopped for precisely "One Mississippi," tonguing the air for molecules.

Now she was rectilining again, quiet as a cougar would have been 400 years before, and in a three-minute span that seemed like forever (yes, obscurely) to the python, she was in position to distinguish, based on the infrared gradient, head from feet. Her hunger was overwhelming, her "understanding" of the body's orientation was absolute, her fear was in check, and it was all systems go. She absolutely rammed the head with a hammering strike of 2.7 meters per second, generating a G-force of 30, or 30 times the force of gravity! It was a perfect bullseye, and quicker than a possum could poop, the first full coil was around the neck.

At the "Three Mississippi" mark, the stunned razorback exhaled its last. The python had pegged him correctly; at 120 pounds he was bigger than Cove, smaller than Jubal and only ten pounds short of the python herself. Oh, what a fine, fine feed he would be! (In python terms, of course.)

Razorbacks, or wild pigs, were the last of the remaining large mammals in Tennessee, along with humans of course. They weren't even natural to the area, but they had out-survived the deer, bear, bobcats, and coyotes. By 2145 they were wild and non-wooly, literally. The variety that survived and evolved had hardly any hair; bare skin could more readily shed their body heat. Biologists had a running bet going—not that any of them would live to pay up—on which would last the longest in Tennessee: *Homo sapiens* or *Sus scrofus*. They seldom talked about it, and when they did, they did so ineffectively, as biologists usually did. No one listened to them.

Meanwhile, in slow motion by human standards, the Cenozoic Era—the Age of Mammals—was coming to a close, certainly in the South and, as long as global heating continued, certainly on Earth. Mesoland was expanding no slower than a python's rectilining. Rectilining straight north, in the USA, and straight south, south of Mesoland. Rectilining relentlessly. Taking over Earth, or at least returning it to the Mesozoic, the Age of Reptiles. The conveyor belts wouldn't stop until the methane ran out.

On this sunny daybreak in July, the python was "satisfied," oh so dimly but oh so very. She was warm, felt no hunger, and had no fear. Few feelings on the planet could be dimmer—relative to a human's—than her feeling of satisfaction. There were at least 88 exceptions, however: the "feelings" (stretching the term to the maximum feasible extent) of the 88 coiled embryos, warm as well in their yolk sacs, soon to be nourished by genuine Tennessee razorback molecules. Described in terms of the "light bulbs" on Earth, theirs were like miniature flashlight bulbs, flickering on a single volt and a single amp.

For the mother python and her 88 embryos, there was no amusement, no imagination, and no aspiration. There was no planning for the future of Earth. There was only this dim satisfaction in the year 2145.

Cincinnati

Ron and Luke rose a little after sunrise, hung over but not horribly. They couldn't afford to sleep in longer, as reports of Heat Wave Ernest had come in over the Tectonicas gathered at the hoedown. Always threateningly hot (and almost always humid in Tennessee), the named heat waves were nothing to fool around with. Ernest would be seeping into Appalachia around the same time the *Midwest Express* would be loading in Nashville, with highs pushing 126 degrees. Luke said, "Better hope the Coldon car is full!"

Rubbing the sleep from his eyes, Ron stifled a crotchety comment about the Coldon Caldors from Tang. He reached for the $130 bottle of water he'd placed near the foot of his T-pad. He was glad the cap was on tight, for somehow it had gotten knocked over during the night. Ron vividly recalled his "Covejule" dream and assumed he must have knocked it over himself. Another bottle between him and the western screen door was knocked over, and Ron had a fleeting thought of some other poor soul with Cove on his mind.

Ron's thoughts quickly shifted to Julia. Now, in the morning and in the rising light of sobriety, he wasn't torn at all. Cove was a beauty, no doubt, and she was sweet in her own right, but nothing about the scenario with Cove made any sense (at least as it might involve Ron), while everything about his future life with Julia made perfect sense. Steeled by the sudden clarity and refreshed by the water, Ron was on the fast road to recovery from his hangover. Luke, meanwhile, was more or less an alcoholic, so he was accustomed to fuzzy mornings.

As the two men and their mules journeyed north, Ron was lost in thought. Julia's treatments in Chicago would end in a week. And then what, exactly? Ron knew only the immediate plan: He and Luke would hole up in the evening at Sara's, set out for Nashville early the next morning, and, assuming SoTrak wasn't mired in Slotrak mode, he'd be clickety-clacking his way to Chicago via Louisville and Cincinnati.

The day went off without a major hitch. The heat was punishing, but that was hardly surprising. At least they were riding north, with the sun at their back.

Frank's wife was manning the Murfreesboro store, so they stopped for water and, this time, some boa jerky that had just arrived from Beechgrove.

Up to now, Ron had managed to steer clear of snake, in the gustatory sense as well as the literal, but the hoedowners had raved about boa in particular, and Ron was hungry as an empty python, so he tried the strip he was offered by the wife. He was nothing short of amazed at the palatability of the serpent. It seemed sort of halfway between fish and chicken (which it sort of was, in an evolutionary sense). While totally de-hydrated—it was jerky after all—it was easy to chew, especially after a bit of salivary moisturizing. It was a mild meat, and like most mild meats, all it needed was a little salt and pepper to turn out fine. This batch of jerky was salted and peppered perfectly, and Ron de-cided to buy two more strips for the ride to Sara's, and five more for the *Midwest Express*. "Beats the heck out of a SoTrak soy stick," he opined between bites.

Luke chuckled affirmatively, "I bet it does, now."

Not much of note transpired on the remaining stretch to Sara's, except for a brief encounter with the Tennessee Game Police. A couple of officers were lean-ing against their truck in the shade of a kudzu-covered eucalyptus, and as the mule riders approached, they could see from their saddles a medium-sized python and a big (in boa terms, at least) boa lying dead in the bed of the truck. Luke asked like a cowboy at a round-up, "Did ya head 'em or heel 'em?"

One of the officers replied, "Funny you should ask, mister. We were just arguin' about that. I say on the python I head-shot 'im. Junior ranger here calls it a tail shot. What say you?"

Luke, as Ron had observed from the moment they'd met, was a diplomatic sort—maybe empathetic even—and he averred, "Well, I can't rightly tell from here, at least not on the python, but looks like you got the head and the tail and everything betwixt on that boa!"

"Got that right," the junior officer chimed in. "Hell, he sent so many pellets through there, half the jerky's gone already!"

As the riders continued up the road, they over-heard another disagreement between the officers. Something to do with counting the snakes. "That one there," the junior officer was saying, "you might as well count as a half, since a half went out with the pellets."

The senior officer argued, "That ain't how I look at it, son. Hell, the way he's almost cut in half there, I could count 'im as two."

The riders reached Sara's place by mid-after-noon, thoroughly wiped out by the heat, humidity, and after-effects of last night's raisin jack (Luke) and spelt beer (Ron). Sara's place had a spring, "clear of chem-icals" she boasted without knowing for sure, and Ron immediately went to it with cupped hands. They hobbled their mounts for the evening, so the mules could move around enough to evade any snakes, and settled into a quiet meal of spelt gruel and kudzu leaves.

Kudzu wasn't anything to brag about, but it was just as edible as collards and infinitely more available. And it was supposed to help against cramps; a constant challenge throughout the Lowmerican climate. Spelt with a side of kudzu was a standard meal in these parts, especially outside of a special occasion (like a hoedown or a brand-new guest), and conducive to a somber meal with little fanfare. Ron thought it apt, this low-key meal, with Heat Wave Ernest coming in earnest.

The next afternoon, as Ron and Luke approached the train station, a sweat-drenched Luke waxed philosophical aboard his mule, "Ron, I never met anyone from as far north as you, and I reckon I never will again." He paused to recall the past three days and managed to summarize the most salient events. "I'm sure glad I spotted you afore you stuck that foot into that forever pond. Julia wouldn't like you limpin' along, one foot good and the other a plastic stump. But we had us a time, Ron; we surely did. You fit right in with the hoedown. You fit right on in. Tell you what, now: Hoodoo's never gonna forget the 'kudzu, crushers, and Jesus Cristo!' HAW, Clem alone'll keep that one afloat! And then when you were dancin' there with Cove, I'd a'guessed the North would never see you again. She's my cousin, you know. Me and you could have ended up in-laws, by God. Or outlaws, knowin' that Cove!

"But then, I didn't just fall off the kudzu cart. I know you gotta get back to that Julia. Don't you ever think it otherwise, either. I heard you torturin' yourself in that bunkhouse: 'Julecove, Covejule' and the like. Why, you were wrigglin' around so much I thought for a second there you was a snake! But from everything you said about Julia, you're good to go, my friend.

"If you ever make it back to these parts, you be sure to bring that woman along, now. And don't you worry about Cove. She's a survivor and she'll have men lined up all the way to Beechgrove."

Luke knew Ron would never "make it back to these parts," much less with his precious Julia, but in this time of parting, his sentiments were relevant, nonetheless.

Ron knew he wouldn't be back again, either. The trip had been an ordeal but, thanks to Luke, it had bolstered him in a way he'd never experienced in the North. It had given him a glimpse into the best of humanity. The folks down here were...how could he describe it... They were real and they were beautiful, yet so ephemeral in the heat, so strong but so susceptible, so close to the Mesoland Containment Corridor. They were truly "at the margin."

And Luke...Luke he'd remember forever. Luke was up there with Alf, among the acquaintances of his 20th year. Julia, Alf, and Luke. Plus a few others like Megan, Jim Kettering, and the Garzas. But Luke was something, now, and Ron felt a tear forming in his right eye. He'd never experienced such a thing in his adult life. Almost right away, another half-tear was palpable in the left eye, too. He had to turn away from Luke and mutter something about watching out for the crushers and the decimators.

The last time he looked at Luke, it was through the fog of a Coldon-smudged window as the *Midwest Express* rolled away from the platform. Damn those Caldors for their Coldon smudging. And what was it the officer Gutierrez had said? "Adios, amigo."

While the trains of the 22nd century could never be considered "cool" in physiological terms or in a sweeping historical context, the *Midwest Express* of July 6, 2145, was so much cooler than the front edge of Ernest (which Ron and his friend Luke had ridden through) that Ron drifted off to sleep before the *Express* made it out of Tennessee. He stayed asleep all the way to Louisville, where the Coldon supply wagon had been washed away in a flash flood the previous evening. In the midst of 125° temperatures and 98 percent humidity, the Express went into Coldon-rationing mode. Any further sleep on the stretch to Cincinnati would be compromised by the discomforts of sweating, stickiness, and stench. But the $140 bottles of water in the dining car made the trip livable.

Ron was starting to wonder why the price of water kept going up. Since he'd left Tang, a bottle of water had risen from $90 to the present price of $140, always increasing and never decreasing. He commented on it to the conductor. An omniscient economist might have identified a hundred factors, but the conductor's one-word response was, "Ernest." As far as one-word responses went, it was good as any, but it left out a few little details such as global heating, the receding Great Lakes, aquifer depletion, river depletion, water pollution, and even sea-level rise (which inundated coastal aquifers with saltwater). And of course, the hydrological contrast between Alaska (especially Anchorage, where water still ran free) and "Mesoland North" explained much of the price differential encountered on Ron's trip to date. From Louisville onward, water would be cheaper again (but not in the long term, as all the "little details" had yet to run their course).

As for Louisville, the SoTrak station was about as busy as Murfreesboro. Between the heat of Ernest and the misery of the recent flood, Kentuckians were holed up in place, truly in survival mode in many cases. They were just one state up from "Mesoland North," meaning only one state stood between them and Mesoland per se. Those privy to an ecological education or those who'd explored a bit—like Ron—either knew about or vaguely suspected the conveyor belts of extinction. But the privy were rare, and most of the explorers were fun seekers, not knowledge seekers.

Ron had no idea how few people were aware of the extinction conveyor belt, but he assumed it was a very small number, because no one had mentioned it besides the Mesoland Agency's Makayla. (He couldn't know it, but precisely six Kentuckians—four from Bowling Green and two from Louisville—had encountered Makayla at the 1907 Tavern in Bowling Green and had heard a mini-lecture about the conveyor belt.) He found it interesting, compelling, and finally disturbing that such a momentous phenomenon was familiar to such a tiny portion of the populace. Not that he thought in terms of "momentous phenomenon" or "portion of the populace." The travel-hardened Ron just concluded, "Shit, nobody knows!"

On the way to Cincinnati, sleep elusive despite the late hours, Ron's thoughts wandered back to the people on Tang. They had everything—power, money, and security—and they could do almost anything they wanted, go wherever they wanted. But they weren't happier than anyone else, or at least anyone who had their basic needs met. They weren't even happier than Luke, Zander, Cove and the rest of the hoedowners who hardly had any needs met. Why not?

Then, on the other side of that general coin, Ron found an irony. The Tangians, with all that wealth failing to make them happier, created a lot of misery for others around the world. They were "greedy"—a word almost never used on Tang but learned by Ron during his travels—as they used far more of the world's materials and energy than anyone else. Ron was only 20, with no particular insights about the "ecological footprint" or the "pollution imprint" of cities and nations, but his nascent common sense had kicked in between the confines of Tang and the expanses of Lowmerica. His fellow Tangians were using vast quantities of resources, surfeited in luxury, while Lowmericans struggled merely to survive. Not just Lowmericans but, to a substantial extent, almost everyone outside of Tang.

The hot stretch between Louisville and Cincinnati became a formative phase in the young Ron Neuwirth's life. A thousand memories from a few dozen days were synthesized into a self-identity that hadn't existed before. The biggest question that demanded attention was: Was he or wasn't he one of the greedy ones? He hailed from Tang, but his heart would never quite fit there again. Not after Julia, Alf, and Luke. Not after this summer of 2145.

The *Express* dropped into the Ohio River Valley toward the end of a waxing moon that was still capable of illuminating a river, a shoreline, and a skyline; all three at once in shadowy contrast. Ron had been awed by the Chugach Mountains near Anchorage, the Olympics as seen from the Space Needle, and the Tetons he'd seen from Yellowstone, but straight ahead was a sight that stirred a nuanced combination of awe, inspiration, and hope. This was no Wyoming, but the distances were sweeping, nonetheless. As with the Missouri and the Mississippi, the Ohio River wasn't what it used to be but, flowing high from recent rains, it rippled with wonder by moonlight. And, as the train rolled into Cincinnati Union Terminal, Ron rolled through the prettiest city he'd seen yet. Unlike Nashville, where the music had died, or New York where the financial district had flooded, Cincinnati seemed comprised of functional, well-maintained houses and businesses. Lanterns and candles were visible from thousands of windows, and none of the neighborhoods seemed run down or vandalized. Nothing was gaudily lit; lighting was tactful and non-obtrusive. People were out walking, biking, scootering, and e-biking, evading the daytime temperatures of Ernest. Kids were playing basketball and couples were strolling the streets. Even some old-timers were out and about; quite a few actually with canes and crutches and wheelchairs. No one was fighting, and no one carried an AR-45.

Ron never thought for a moment, "This is nice; this is functional. Democracy actually worked here." His thoughts weren't that explicit. Yet the people and the scenery of Cincinnati did inspire him with vague hopes for a humanity somewhere between the excesses of Tang and the impoverishment of Hoodoo.

Cincinnati became the Luke of cities for Ron. He'd never know it well, but what he knew of it, he loved, and he'd always think kindly of it.

At long last, Ron was on the final stretch of his eastern-southern, fact-finding, impression-gathering journey. The *Midwest Express* was headed to Chicago with a partial supply of Coldon, an ample selection of soy sticks, and a fully enthusiastic Ron Neuwirth, ready to re-convene with his gentle, genuine Julia.

The Proposal

The kiss evoked from Ron the strongest feelings he'd ever had. With Julia in his arms, right there on the platform of Terminal 22, at the uncrowded end away from the concourse, he proposed to her. "You're all I'll ever want, Julia," he said sincerely as he brought out the pearl earrings from Sandy Hook Bay. He'd never been more focused and, unlike at the hoedown bunkhouse, his mind was entirely free of anxiety or doubt.

Alas, he'd never be more confused, either, than he was by Julia's reaction, "We have to talk, Ron." She looked fraught with worry; he put the earrings back in his pocket.

They went to a coppee stand in the concourse and, waiting in line, Julia seemed distant and preoccupied, staring up at the menu sign but with eyes searching beyond it. Ron was no psychotherapist, but he was perceptive enough to know that something other than the coppee menu was plaguing Julia. He was starting to wonder if her treatments hadn't worked, if she was dying despite all the efforts of Northwestern Memorial. She looked kind of pale, but the reasons were as of yet obscure.

When they'd taken their coppee to an empty gate across the concourse, Ron twisted sideways in his seat, sideways to face her, and asked, "Are you ok, honey?"

"Yes, yes Ron, I'm okay. The treatments worked."

Julia glanced down at her coppee, then up at Ron, and then back down again at the coppee. She stared at the coppee for a good half minute and adjusted the coppee, while Ron waited patiently for whatever was coming. She stared at the cup in her hands for a few seconds more and finally asked, without looking up, "Do you know Lu Ming?"

Ron was stunned. How would Lu Ming possibly enter into the picture? He replied, "Lu Ming?"

Julia turned to look straight at Ron. Her blue eyes were blurred by moisture, and the rest of her face was tightened in anxiety. Finally, she confessed, "Oh Ron, I'm so, so sorry. I hate this moment and I don't know exactly how to tell you this, but..." she paused for several seconds... "Lu Ming hired me to spy on you."

Ron suddenly felt like the sole operator of a small

ship whose anchor was proving too small for the task, bumping along at the bottom, and threatening to let him loose in the choppy waves of the Bering Sea. He tested the emotional bottoms for some purchase and found it with a sense of relief. For one thing, she'd confided in him, revealing a profoundly important truth, and vigorously apologizing in the process. More importantly, she hadn't given any bad news about her medical condition. For clarification he asked, "Are *you* okay? Are the treatments working?" Only then he thought to ask, "I mean, you are actually receiving treatments, right?"

A half-developed look of relief appeared on Julia's face, too, and she explained, "Oh Ron, yes, I got the treatments and they worked, but that's how Lu Ming got me into this thing. He knew I needed to come down here. He'd been following you from Tang and he tracked you to the Conveners meetings.

"Ron, I'm so sorry, but this thing with my condition...I was in real trouble. The treatments aren't free—they're not cheap either—and there's no way I could have managed it with the Fantaste job.

"Oh Ron, Lu Ming showed up at the flat one day and offered to pay for not only my treatments but for all the travel, the missed wages, the rent, and every-thing. He promised he wasn't intending to hurt you, either. *I swear,* Ron, otherwise I wouldn't have done it! He just said, 'Keep an eye on him, let me know where he is, and tell me what he says.' He gave me a new Tectonica just for the job, programmed with a T-function straight to him. I really needed one, too, and he cleared out the T-bill from my old one. But then, as he was leaving, he said he'd be keeping an eye on me as well, and if I failed to follow through... well then, he might do something to you, and maybe to me as well!

"It really scared me, Ron, and I figured from then on, I was being watched or at least monitored with the Tectonica. That's why I said I needed to meet you in person! I shut it off when we meet, you know. Most of the time at least. I'm assuming he can still track my location with it, but he can't hear us with the thing turned off and stuffed away in my pack, right?"

Ron had no idea, either, but Julia's revelation had finally solved at least one mystery, as he had indeed wondered, ever since Julia had arrived in Chicago weeks ago, why she'd insisted on meeting in person. She'd said, as he recalled, "There's some stuff I have to tell you, and it had to be in person." Yet everything she'd said afterward would have been totally transmittable by Tectonica. But the linkage to Lu Ming changed the equation. Yes, to be safe, the things Julia was telling him now would have to be conveyed in person.

Conversely, the Lu Ming linkage to Julia explained why Ron hadn't seen Ming—as far as he knew—since his swing through Seattle. From Chicago on, Ron's movements and main activities would have been relayed by Julia, and as for the "kind of short and stocky" fellow spotted by Norma at the 60th St. theatre...who knew? Perhaps Ming occasionally supplemented Julia's "spycraft" with other of his agents and associates. More likely it was just one of the random passersby Norma also mentioned.

With these mysteries solved, or solved enough for Ron's satisfaction, his anchor was finding purchase again, and the seas were settling around him. He experienced and made note of the fact that he was largely unscathed and unfazed by the Lu Ming-Julia linkage. In fact, he'd found yet another source of relief because, if it hadn't been for Lu Ming's "need to know," Julia may have never received her treatments. "Everything happens for a reason," Maritza Garza had said once over a Plastic Plaza dinner, and if ever there was a case in point, this was it.

"Well, young lady," he finally said to the six-month younger beauty, "you still have a question to answer." Julia was looking less worried now, but quizzical, so Ron pulled the earrings back out and dangled them before her eyes.

The quizzical look disappeared, replaced by a beaming smile Ron would never forget, as Julia hugged him with an also-unforgettable "Yes!" They kissed, for the first time with the passion of lovers, right there in the chairs of Gate 6. Julia donned the earrings (a standard symbol of marriage popularized by the T-Tokkers

Zeke and Lacey), and now she looked like an angel adorned. The two stood up and kissed again.

They couldn't spend the rest of the day kissing at Gate 6, though, and finally Ron said, "I have an idea. Turn that Tectonica back on and let's do the proposal part again! Then let's grab the next train back to Seattle. My dad shot me another $80,000 of T-credits on the way here from Cincinnati. That's enough for us to get one of those sleeper cars, and we can figure out our plan from the dining car when you 'forget' to bring the Tectonica."

It was a fuzzy plan, hastily contrived and bare bones at best, but it had a lot of advantages, starting with the reenactment of their marriage vows, complete with a repeat of the passionate kissing. And, if Lu Ming or his information processors were listening, surely they'd conclude that Ron had "settled down" and chosen a life of domestic bliss—or at least a stage of it—rather than revolutionary proselytizing. Which was true, including the "stage" part most likely. Just to be safe, though, they'd travel forthwith rather than actually "settle" in Chicago where they could easily be found. The goal for now was to make it to Tang before they might be detained or interrogated.

On the other hand, Ron did have a revolutionary spirit, or at least a level-headed predisposition for reform. He was a sincere young man, too, and literally not capable of putting on much of an act. Neither was

Julia, for that matter. So that night in the dining car of the *Western Zephyr*, they devised a plan. They would (in addition to their west-bound honeymooning, of course) keep the Tectonica running most of the time, and they'd have lengthy discussions about Ron's travels and Julia's treatments. Ron, especially, would be "pushing the envelope," as the ancient saying went, by describing how miserable the conditions were for the vast majority of people almost everywhere he'd been. Ron really wanted Lu Ming to know—because just maybe he didn't know already—what the world had come to outside of Tang. Lu Ming ought to discover exactly who and what he was working for. It was entirely possible that he "knew" the individuals comprising the 100—Swintons, Caldors, Trembults and the like—but didn't really *know* them and what they stood for. Ron wanted Lu Ming to see the contrast between the 100 and the struggling families off Tang like the Nobles, Garzas, and Perrins.

The newlywed couple would keep these conversations running the whole way back to Tang: on the *Zephyr*, the *Sandra Lopez*, and the *Chakirya*. They'd keep their stays in Seattle and Anchorage to the minimum possible. Conceivably they could avoid hotel stays in both cities, although it would be cutting it close for catching the *Chakirya*. With a little luck, they'd arrive in Tang by the 20th of July.

And so it went that, day after day for the next ten

of them, Ron described at length the people, places, concepts, and principles he'd learned about. All of it was fresh in his youthful memory, so Lu Ming would get an earful about the rafts of waste at sea, the stench of Puget Sound, the devastating poverty of Containerville, the dangerous desperados south of Yellowstone, the oppressive dry heat of Neo-Mexico, the brutalizing humidity of "Mesoland North"—heat everywhere aside from Tang (so far)—the forever chemicals in the water supply of Chicago, the plastic particulates in the rain downwind of every major city, the gun violence in New York, the homeless trampling of Central Park, the "haircut" mountains of West Virginia, the flat-hillbillies living in abandoned mines, the kudzu-covering of practically anything standing south of Ohio...on and on he would talk.

Meanwhile, the intelligent, perceptive Julia, with her self-education in conservation, would interject with questions and observations about pollutants, diseases, and invasive species. One day on the *Sandra Lopez*, her prompting led to an entire afternoon devoted to the topics of Mesoland, the Containment Corridor, and Mesoland North. Ron recalled and relayed the concepts he'd picked up from Makayla, especially, about the molecular clock, trophic levels, and, most of all, the conveyor belt of extinction. At one point in the conversation, with the Tectonica positioned for perfect transmission, Julia asked the profoundly disturbing question, "When does it stop?" That opened the door to a lengthy discussion of global heating, the methane feedback loop, and the "ecological unravelling" that came with the incessant push for a higher GDP.

The nights, of course, were devoted to an entirely different activity; this was nobody's business except for the pair of passionate newlyweds.

Lu Ming

Lu Ming was nothing if not curious. A 53-year-old descendant of immigrants who'd come to Seattle from China during the Wasteful, he was perhaps the brightest of a long line of scientists, researchers, and tech-savvy operators. His grandfather had been recruited for naval intelligence, and his father became a satellite communications engineer, stationed on Tang from 2103 until his death in 2129. Lu Ming grew up alongside the 100, who quickly took over Tang and set about securing it for themselves. They hired Lu to oversee Northland Security. Technically, Lu's boss was Rentz Trembult, Jr., the chairman of the board, but in day-to-day operations, Lu called the shots.

Lu was expected not only to direct the technical operations of Northland—including the massive Tier

Line program—but to use these technical abilities to squelch any opposition to the 100 (Trembults, Caldors, and all the rest). Opposition could come in many forms, and before it could be squelched it had to be detected and understood, so Lu had developed an intelligence agency that operated on Tang and, as needed, in various cities of the world.

One particular element of opposition that arose at times was the phenomenon of "rogue natives." These were Tangians—invariably in their teens or twenties and usually male—who developed a scornful attitude toward the 100, starting typically with their own parents. Usually, it didn't amount to much beyond a phase of unfocused rebellion. A rebel without a cause might act foolishly and behave recklessly, but frankly the families of Tang didn't care, unless the rebel went off-island and turned into a radical or a revolutionary, castigating the 100 in public venues such as T-sites, the plastipapers, or even theatres. Lu didn't allow for such shenanigans, and he'd eliminated several rogues, usually with the help of his agents but on two occasions himself (both times by poison).

Yet Lu was never comfortable with killing. The effects were unpredictable, it was heavy-handed and wasteful, and, somehow, it just seemed wrong in a way he couldn't quite place. He avoided it if at all possible.

When the young Ron Neuwirth was rumored to be curious about the world beyond Tang, Lu didn't overreact. Curiosity was something they had in common. In Lu's case, though, it hadn't ever led to an exploration of the lands and peoples beyond Tang. His geographic knowledge had been developed almost exclusively for purposes of placing agents where he needed them to intercept or monitor Tangian rogues or other opponents. It's not that he was disinterested in places and peoples, but the demands of his technical and intelligence work kept him fully occupied and, in many cases, fascinated.

On the other hand, he wasn't oblivious to the overlap. He knew that threats could arise from any number of places, people, and events. Recently he'd taken some interest, for example, in the environmental issues that seemed to be pushing people to and from different parts of the world. He was an ecological neophyte, but he was logical to a fault, and he could connect the dots when they appeared.

With Ron Neuwirth, then, Lu Ming expanded his horizons and took a new approach. While he was wary of Ron, he actually encouraged Skyler, Ron's father (whom he'd played with as a child), to send the young man off to explore. He'd manage to monitor Ron's activities with a combination of input from Skyler, agents in the bigger cities, and Tectonica tracers. When Skyler became engrossed in a major business deal, taking all of his time in the last weeks of June, Lu took matters into his own hands and infiltrated Ron's nascent net-

work in Anchorage. He picked up on the budding relationship with Julia, and watched them with binoculars
for nearly an hour from a hill above the conservation
center. T-records from the Anchorage Tectonica server revealed her medical condition, and within a week,
Lu recruited her with the assurance he would do Ron
no harm. That was indeed Lu's intent, to do no harm
(within reason, of course).

Lu was no python, dimly lit and barely sensing.
He had the complete human package of acute sensory perception and conception, with neurons firing
like sparklers at a fireworks display. Unlike a display,
though, and relative to others on Tang, he was inscrutable. He was fully aware of this trait, too; aware as well
that he was "supposed" to be inscrutable, pursuant to
stereotype. He played it up for all it was worth and, unbeknownst to all but his wife, had fun with it, cracking
wry jokes with her about it on occasion.

No, Lu was not a humorless man, inscrutability
notwithstanding, and he found himself chuckling to
himself more than once about the trials and tribulations of young Ron the explorer. He'd only picked
up bits and pieces of the Tennessee portion of Ron's
trip—and those were blurred and perhaps inaccurate—
but the thought of the lad riding a crotchety old mule,
sweating on the edge of the Ernest heat wave, hung
over it seemed from some kind of moonshine... while
not hilarious, it fit with the droll humor he appreciated.

Lu was mildly tickled, too, by the notions Ron and Julia seemed to share about him. They must have really thought him a curmudgeon; a curmudgeon and a killer. They were afraid of him, with a fear that neither delighted nor dismayed Lu, but caused him to intro-spect nonetheless. He *had* been a killer, directly and indirectly, and each time he'd killed or ordered a killing, he'd detected a little loss of life himself. Now he found himself hoping, wishing, that smart people like Ron and Julia didn't detest him, or wouldn't detest him if they knew all he'd done. Still, he'd had a job to do, and for all he originally knew, Ron could have gone rogue indeed; gone off the deep end and caused a great deal of damage to the interests of Tang. For example, he could have attempted to bring back one of the "foot-print investigators" he'd heard about; T-hackers who'd write about the luxuries and the wanton waste on Tang, stirring up talk of taxes or oven takeover.

There were, now and then, red flags about Ron's developing sense of social justice, but nothing crazy enough to warrant a "disinfection campaign," much less elimination. Lu found himself thankful that nothing of the sort would be called for, apparently. Meanwhile, he was picking up bits and pieces of important infor-mation pertaining to "security at large," as he'd started to call it. The 100 might manage to keep the people of the planet at bay, and keep them as customers for their GDP, but to what end if, in the process, they burned a hole through the foundation of their very existence?

Lu had a son, too. Li Ming was four years younger than Ron, forming opinions, developing attitudes, withstanding emotions, and exploring the world via Tectonica. Tectonicas were as powerful as the corporation that spawned them, but (as Lu knew so well) they hardly provided for a worldly education. One of Lu's own programs, "T-Tightening" they called it in-house, was designed precisely to mold public opinion into a manner conducive to sales and implicit approval of the "newest Tang dynasty" (as distinguished from the archaic "New Tang Dynasty" television network of the early Wasteful). Lu had not been able to establish firm control the T-Tightening program, as the Tectonica Corporation had the final say over Tectonica algorithms, and Lu found himself frustrated at times when Li would spend hours on the "Tonic" with nothing to show at the end except a few giggles and a desire to purchase more gear from Plastiwear, Zippercraft, or Tectonica itself.

Now, in the afternoon of July 20, 2145, the *Chakirya* was pulling into port, delivering the freshly minted couple of Ron and Julia Neuwirth. He'd been listening to the pair for weeks; first as individuals and then as a couple. Not that he sat and listened every time they talked—not by a long shot—but he had all the recordings and filtered them every evening for red-flag words and "trouble tips," which the intelligence algorithms identified based on particular emotive frequencies.

And, what he'd found himself doing since the couple left Chicago was actually listening in real time to their discussions; as much as he could find the time for. Oh, he'd figured out that they were staging these, that they fully intended him to listen and "take notes." The thing was, they were onto something. He found himself wanting to listen and take notes, mentally if not literally. He was astounded by the dangers of the nuclear waste at Containerville, the carnage deified at the NRA Towers, the fungal infections inflicting the remainder of New Jersey, and the whole concept of "invasive species," including the pythons and boas flowing relentlessly across the Containment Corridor, never quite contained. It seemed like there were just too many problems: big-picture, overwhelming problems that needed not only the attention of New York, Chicago, Denver and Seattle, but all the world. Any number of these problems could spiral out of control and pose the proverbial "existential threat" to the Upper USA, Alaska, and Tang itself.

The ones that really riveted Lu Ming and started to keep him up at night were global heating, the methane feedback loop, the expansion of Mesoland, and the conveyor belt of extinction. And, there was no doubt that the professor from Columbia, Kettering, was correct in his assessment that almost all these problems were driven by the growing GDP. Neurons firing a mile a minute, Ming was connecting the dots left and right now. Big dots and little dots, short lines and long lines, causes and effects, costs and benefits, todays and tomorrows for Lu and Li and humanity itself.

As the *Chakirya* pulled into port, Lu Ming made himself fully visible along the railing. He wanted to witness whatever reaction Ron would have to him, first-hand and close up. Julia came first across the gangway; Ron right behind her. She was the first one to spot him, and her gait became noticeably slower and stiffer. She nervously glanced behind herself at Ron, then back at Lu. Now Ron's gaze met Lu's, but there was no sign of fear and no noticeable physical reaction. In the shuffling of the departing passengers, Ron came abreast of Julia and took her hand, and a few seconds later they passed Lu Ming, who watched them more out of personal curiosity than professional scrutiny. None of them said a word, and Ming remained expressionless until the couple was off the zipper and into a pedicab.

Some days went by before Lu Ming encountered Ron again. These were blissful days for Ron and Julia; blissful and busy, too, with all the catching up that comes after the return of an adventurous son. Julia was a big part of the catching up, of course, and she adjusted quickly and naturally to her new surroundings and new family. What lay ahead was very, very many hours and days, weeks and months and years of reconciling

Ron's findings—and frankly Julia's life experience—with the political and economic facts and circumstances of Tang. From 2145 onward, it was a work in progress, with Ron and Julia playing leading roles in a reform movement, the outcome of which is yet to be determined.

Meanwhile, on July 26 to be precise, not even a week after the couple's arrival, Ron and Lu Ming met in person for the first time (their passage at port notwithstanding). Ron was in his customary contemplation spot, surely thinking of life ahead with Julia, legs dangled over the same cliff Ming had seen him at dozens of times over the years. Lu Ming made his appearance slowly and from a distance—about 30 feet to the right of Ron—so as not to startle Ron, who was, after all, along the edge of a cliff. It would be one of the few times they'd talk, and the conversation was brief. Ron said politely, almost formally, "How do you do, Mr. Ming?" He wasn't entirely without fear, but he wasn't panicked either, so he kept his legs dangled over the cliff. Ming was acting in a non-threatening manner, keeping his distance. Besides, Ron thought, if Lu Ming wanted him dead, it either would have happened by now, or it would happen soon enough.

Lu Ming replied, "Mr. Neuwirth, see that zipper?" He was looking in binoculars at the *Sprite*, a zipper rumored to be transporting Heraldine Leonard and her crew of resource locators to a suspected lithium deposit across the Bering Sea in Siberia.

Ron answered with a question, "Is that the one heading to Siberia? Julia was telling me that lithium deposit is in the last remaining wood-bison forest on Earth." He instantly regretted mentioning Julia, and especially her knowledge of the bison (which she'd acquired from the conservation center). Her knowledge, and the fact that she might be talking about it, was precisely the type of thing Lu Ming might want to "disinfect."

Lu Ming lowered his binoculars, letting them hang next to his sternum. Along his belt were three Tectonicas, one of which he selected and pointed northwest, up into the sky. The answering of questions with further questions continued, as Ming posed another one, "And the T-59 Satellite?" Ron and everyone else had heard about numerous numbered satellites, but he had no idea what #59 was for.

Standing at an angle—looking partly toward Ron and partly toward the *Sprite*—Ming manipulated a few buttons on the Tectonica, then looked straight at Ron and slowly announced, "Yes, she's heading to Siberia. But don't worry; she won't be finding any lithium. I'll be the one sending the T-59 signals." He paused for a moment and added, "You didn't hear that."

Lu Ming's face was as expressionless as a plasti-block. Then he winked and walked away.

About the Author

Peter Seidel holds a B.S. in Architectural Engineering from the University of Colorado and a Masters in Architectural Planning from the Illi-nois Institute of Technology where he studied under renowned architect, Mies van der Rohe. Seidel has served as a faculty member at the University of Michigan and Virginia Tech, and he also taught at Central China Institute of Science and Technology. His work has been published in numerous academic journals and he has also authored four other books: *2045*, *Invisible Walls*, *Global Survival*, and *Uncommon Sense.*